Blu is in the Rainbow, Too!

Chapter One

It was one of the hottest days of the summer and I was sitting on the car-porch rubbing ice cubes on my knees until the ice melted, trying to stay cool. "Granma, how can you stand to be in that kitchen as hot as it is?" I have lived in the South my whole life. You would think I'd be used to this humidity every summer.

"Blu?"

"Yes, Granma?"

"While you out there daydreaming you could be in here helping me finish up my Sunday dinner for tomorrow."

Little does she know, I'm sitting out here thinking I'm pretty certain I am pregnant and wishing I had someone I could talk to about it. I'm so scared, I'm not close at all to my mom. I have two older sisters and two younger brothers. My brothers are with "family". My sisters are doing there on thing, wherever that is. We all have different dads but my granma took to me as if I were an only child. It actually makes me feel closest to her. I want to put aside my fear and tell my mom I'm pregnant, but she only seems to want to get involved in my life when she sees the chance to put me down or take charge of a situation that she clearly has nothing to do with. The list goes on with her. My boyfriend drives up as I'm in deep thought. All of a sudden, I hear his voice all upbeat and happy.

"Hey, why you sitting out here in this heat like this?"

Oh, hey. Oh Hey, is all I get? I'm sorry, I got a lot on my mind.

"Yeah, I know. Your mind was definitely somewhere else. I came over here to see you because I was thinking this is a good time to go tell your mom the news, even if I have to tell her. I'll take her head on since you so scared. Besides, you got to be about three or four months by now and gonna start showing soon."

"Hell I may be about five months. I really don't know. But I do know I need to go to the doctor and fast."

"Ya think?" Thadius raised his eyebrows but his eyes had kindness shining through. "Okay, so when you going?"

"Don't know. I really don't know the first move I need to make." He shouted out,"I do, and that's tell your mom." I hesitated but then said "Okay, let's go." But I'm telling you now that she is going to act a fool on us in the worst way. You know we don't get along, and she hates you." Thadius held me close to his chest to comfort me. Just being around him made my heart flutter.

He's 6'6 weighs about 225 pounds. His skin is the color of coffee with a splash of cream. He stays in the gym and muscles are all over his body. He has a low hair cut and his eyes are a dreamy dark brown.

His body chemistry with cologne is impeccable. Initially, he complimented my hair. The length is midway of my back, with deep waves of curls. My mother is Italian and white and my father is black. I have a light complexion. I'm 5'10 and my weight is between 135 and 140 pounds. Thad always says, "Girl, thank God for hips, because yours are perfect." So he thought. My eyes are light brown. He says I have the most kissable lips. I usually wear fitted jeans and some type of blouse that shows just enough cleavage. Now that I'm pregnant, my wardrobe has drastically changed. I stay in t-shirts and I've even borrowed pants from the girl who lives two houses down. She's about two sizes bigger than me. People always say I'm a younger version of my mom. She is so beautiful, but mean as hell. Just out right bitter, in my opinion. My mom and dad were together off and on, then he was gone and to this day I don't have a clear understanding of all that. I know he lives on the other side of town. I do talk to him on the phone but never see him because he says he travels a lot. He's always told me he would come to see me soon as he could.

We just pulled up outside my moms house. Thad said,

"Alright now, when we get inside I will do all the talking because you look like you about to shit bricks."

Before I knew it I yelled, Wait!

Thad said Why?

Let's just tell her when it's too late to do anything about it.

"He aggressively said No Blu, Ring the doorbell."

"You crazy. Why don't you ring it?"

"Well hell, it's yo mamma."

After standing at the door for what seemed like eternity, I finally heard her voice.

"Who is it?"

"It's me, mamma."

"Girl, where's your key? Oh, hey Thad."

"How you doing, Ms. Cora?"

"Uh huh. Anyway, what y'all up to?"

As if he was holding his breathe or something Thad blurted out, "Ms. Cora, Blu is pregnant."

Well damn, Thad, you sure know how to break it gently. Mamma got up and lit a cigarette. She took two puffs and said "Oh honey, you not bringing no baby in this world. I'm not fixin' to raise nobody baby." (As if she raised me.) "So I say what will or won't happen. And while we on the subject, Mr. Thad, you can leave. I got this from here on out." In the most compassionate tone, he said

"But I don't wanna leave her. Whatever we come up with, I wanna be there."

Mamma roll her eyes and said, "Don't call, don't write, don't do nothing, y'all have done enough." She slammed the door in his face. I was devastated because I hated to deal with any of this without him.

"We taking care of this first thing in the morning."

"Mamma, tomorrow is Sunday!"

"You know what I mean, Monday then. You can go in your room and stay there, because come Monday this will all be over."

I laid in the bed feeling all kind of stuff. Hurt, sickness in my stomach, confusion, anger and other things I can't put a name on. I guess I fell asleep at some point. A cramp, and the sun, woke me up the next morning. I got up to pee then went back and got in the bed. I got back up and drank a lil water from the bathroom sink, only to have it come right back up five minutes later, followed by a minute of gagging. I thought to myself, "What the hell is this about?" That night I was in and out of sleep all night. I had to have fallen off to sleep around five a.m. when I heard a voice with attitude say, "Get up, and let's go." I'm feeling nauseous while riding in this car with Cora. I assume you're not suppose to have food or drink after midnight. It doesn't matter because I haven't been eating anyway. It's complete silence in the car. The radio is not on and it's hot as hell already.

"Fill out this form, young lady. I need for you to give a urine specimen in the cup."

"I will fill the form out, Blu. You just go pee in the cup."

After about thirty minutes, I see that we're leaving. The same thing happen at the next doctor's office, and the third one. Mamma is driving really fast and I'm getting sick.

"Girl, these people say you well over five months. How far along are you?"

"I don't know, but that sounds about right."

"Hell no! You not having no baby. You can forget that. I got to go home and make some more calls."

It just dawned on me that I haven't ate anything since Saturday morning and it's Monday, but I refuse to ask her for anything. She knows good and well I haven't ate. That whole week went by. I stayed out of eyesight of Cora and ate crackers and drank water. She never offered anything to eat and I didn't ask. My stomach isn't big at all. If I didn't feel the baby moving and wasn't so sick I wouldn't know I was pregnant, my stomach is so small.

By Saturday evening I couldn't do it any longer. "Mamma, you got anything I can eat?"

"Yeah, but when you eat that baby grows more and more, you already up in the months where this is going to be expensive."

Anyway, I ate some eggs and toast and went to sleep. The next day we arrived at the clinic, first thing.

"How are you ladies on this Monday morning?" We both looked at the receptionist like, *how do you think we are?* When Mamma finished my paperwork I had to get an ultrasound. After my exam we sat in a little briefing room and waited on the nurse. She came in and said, "You are right at seven months pregnant, Ms. Spencer!"

"What the hell you mean she's seven months?" Mamma said in a nasty tone.

The nurse had a look like, *I know you heard me.*

"Well, is it any way she still can have this abortion?"

The nurse asked to see mamma privately.

Cora signed all the papers and read all the material. I was nothing at this point but a puppet on a string doing whatever she said. It's been this way my whole life, with everything. Cora always said she never wanted kids. The staff told Cora they would be able to do this "procedure" as they called it. "But Blu will have to stay overnight and it's high risk." She agreed to the terms.

Once I got my hospital ID bracelet, gown to change in and instructions to wait in this room by some elevators, Mamma said, "Okay,

see you tomorrow," and left. I'm sitting in
this room with my mind bothered by the fact
that they told Cora that this is a high-risk
procedure and she had to sign a waiver
stating that it's a fifty percent chance
that I could die and they have to be free
and clear of any liabilities. Her words
were, "I don't care cause she not gonna
embarrass me with all this baby nonsense."

"Okay young lady, you ready to go upstairs?
This is your room. Get undressed completely
and put on the gown and socks, and I'll be
back shortly." After I had been waiting
about an hour the nurse came and got me. We
went to what looked like a small operating
room. The nurse and nurse's aide helped me
onto a table. I start panicking. I couldn't
be still for nothing in the world. The nurse

pull some straps from somewhere underneath me. She and the nurse's aide strapped my arms down, then strapped my legs in the stirrups. After a short pause, I heard

"Well hello! I'm Doctor Gresham. It'll be okay, sweetheart. Just take some deep breaths. Now, you're going to feel some pressure, but hold on, it'll only be for a minute." It felt more like an hour. He held four rods in his hand. They look like shotgun shells that were glued together. The doctor inserted them into my vagina. He then picked up a large needle attached to a syringe. "Okay, Ms. Spencer, you're going to feel a pinch in your lower abdomen." He lied. It was more like a stab. That was some kind of shot in my stomach. I kept quiet. I'd never felt anything so painful before.

"Let's return to your room, Blu. Take your time getting in the wheelchair." The nurse took me back to my room. "Blu, let me take a moment and explain to you what's about to happen. First, I want you to lay back and relax, and listen to me good. You're going to go through the same procedure as if you were having a baby, but it will be dead instead of alive."

At that moment I felt pain in my heart, not knowing—or should I say, understanding—what the hurt really was. It just was a pain that had me thinking, *Is this what you feel when somebody dies?*

Another nurse came in to start an IV. "Ms. Spencer, you need the IV to start your contractions. If they didn't tell you already, the rods they inserted are to help you dilate, and the shot you were given in your stomach was similar to acid, to stop the fetus's heart." I was thinking that this bitch should've taken some sensitivity classes while she was in nursing school!

"There you go, young lady. Now, just lie back and nature will take its course."

It's about 12:30 a.m. I drifted off to sleep not knowing I was about to be awakened by a sharp pain going through my stomach. I sat up, my heart racing. My hands are cold and clammy. A few minutes later I felt it again. I buzzed the nurse. She came in and said, "Oh, honey, those are contractions. And don't forget, if you feel like pushing then go ahead, because your rods are coming out first. Then you'll be ready to push the baby out."

I laid back down. I'm hurting more and the pain is sharp, intense and constant. I'm

crying now, and it don't help at all that
I'm alone. I got thoughts that I'm about to
die. It's around 5:30 a.m. I'm in a lot of
pain. My eyes are so swollen from crying, it
hurts when I blink. I feel a lot of pressure
in my lower back. I felt the urge to push,
so I did, pushing again, and then a third
time. Something came out. I was scared to
look cause I was told not to look down
because the baby would be dead instead of
alive and won't look like normal. I looked
anyway. It was the rods. The nurse came and
removed them. She reminded me that the baby
would soon follow. A while went by and the
pain became unbearable. The urge to push is
stronger than ever. I pushed and I pushed.
Something came out but I can still feel it
halfway inside of me so I pulled it the rest
of the way with my hand. I pressed the
button for the nurse. She came in and said,

"That's it." Wrapped it up and put it in a bag. As she walked toward the door, I said, "Can I see?"

"Oh, baby, you don't need to see. But I'll tell you what it is. It's a boy!"

I sat in disbelief for a minute then laid down and asked for something to help me sleep. The nurse told me I had about four hours to rest. I shook my head as if I'm saying OK. After sleeping a while I got up still throwed off from it all, got dressed, got my medication, and walked slowly to the nearest bus stop. Cora had conveniently left bus fare at the front desk. While I sat on the bench waiting on the bus I felt like I was in this world alone. I felt like I just killed my child so I hung my head down and couldn't lift it for nothing. I heard a voice say, you getting on the bus? I looked up and saw the bus driver smiling and waiting patiently while I paid my fair and sat down. Oh how I wish this bus was taking me far away from here. Granma house is going to have to do for now. I'm trying to think back on where it began or should I say when I noticed my mom not caring much for me. I've never seen my mom and dad friendly towards one another. As a small child she never interacted with me. Her attitude always came off like I despise her. During the brief times I lived with her she made me stay in my room and told me to stay out of her way. I never knew and still not sure why I irritated her so much. I asked her when I was about Thirteen years old, mamma why don't you like me? She said, girl I don't like nobody now go on and leave me alone. I never asked her anything else, ever again.

Chapter Two

"**I got us** a hotel room. I wanted to get it for the whole weekend, but we just chilling from Saturday to Sunday."

"What you do that for? I told you I'm not ready yet. Damn, Thad, I just went through some real shit. I mean, give me time."

"Time! What the hell you mean, time? It's been almost three months."

"Yeah, well, I'm not ready."

"See, this that shit I be talking about. Blu, who you fucking?"

"Don't start, okay? You the first and the only, so let that go. Please! Oh, by the way, me and the girls going to Monica's party at the plaza next weekend."

"You mean you and the Hoe's? I can think of two of them that I can have."

"Yeah, well, let you tell it. All my friends want you."

"They do! And you're not going, because what kind of party you going to that your man can't attend?"

"It's a beauty makeover party. People selling lingerie, makeup, sex toys, and just eating and talking. You know, stuff like that."

My mind is soaring into anger. I'm so tired of him. He so possessive and controlling. All this time I was thinking, well, hell, I really don't know what I was thinking. But one thing for sure, I jumped right out the pot from Cora into the fire with his ass. We been together now for a few years. After that pregnancy he has become more and more controlling. Since when does he say I can and can't do something? Before I knew it, my naive ass was asking permission to do anything. He had total control and we weren't even living in the same house. Thad was living at home with his parents and I live with my grandmother because living with Mamma was never a good idea.

"So anyway, Thad, I am going. And while we on the subject, let's just take a break from each other. I been in this relationship like I'm married or something. We young. Hell, I been committed to only you since the beginning. You are so mean, and I'm so miserable. Yes, let's take a break! Go out with other people, and if it's meant to be then we will find our way back to each other."

"Girl, please. I wish I would see you doing anything anywhere."

"So what you saying, Thadius?

"Figure it out. It'll come to you or maybe it won't. Blu, I'm outta here."

"So, we friends, right?"

"Wrong, girl!"

"Well, whatever. Bye, Thad."

The anticipation of going on a date was exciting, yet a little scary because I've only been with one person. Guys always tried to talk to me, and I would always say I got a man. Guys wanted to take me out to all kinds of places, but never would I accept. I wanted to, but was afraid of the unknown with Thad. My friends would always say, "Blu, he's a control freak. He show all signs of being abusive." They would say everything, but I would always come to his defense, knowing they were telling the truth.

"Hello...may I speak to Blu?"

"This she!"

"How you doing, beautiful?

"I'm okay Brent, how you doing?"

"I'm good, but it was hell getting your number from your girl."

"Yeah, I heard you had asked about me again and wanted to get in touch, so I told Carmen she could give you my number."

"I haven't seen you in so long, and we've never really had the chance to talk."

"Well, you know how that go, right?"

"Yeah, you were with that dude, but I never forgot you. Every time I saw you, you look so sad. I would just say, 'Damn, she can't be happy. I don't know what's up, but if I ever get the opportunity to talk with her, I'm gone jump on it.' And it seems the opportunity definitely has presented itself."

"Yep! Seems that way, don't it."

"Well, Ms. Blu, I was thinking we would go to Six Flags this Friday."

"Why Six Flags? And why on a Friday?"

"I was thinking Six Flags because it's carefree, fun, and open, and on Friday cause it's less crowded. Blu, you seem like you need to just let go and have some fun and laughs. Trust me, we will have the best time."

"Okay, sounds good, Brent. See you Friday."

"Cool, I will pick you up at 10 a.m. so we can have all day."

"All right, bye."

He is right on time. Brent, you early but that's cool. Let's Go! As we approached the entrance I couldn't help but be excited and wondering what are we riding first? I could smell the funnel cakes and all kinds of treats in the air. Brent held my waist from behind while we stand in line for a ride. We started at the front of the park and rode everything. I was scared as hell on some of the rides but rode anyway. It was magician shows, all kinds of different entertainment to watch. It felt so carefree just like Brent said it would be. I saw a lot of couples without children having a great time. It almost felt like adult day at Six Flags. I said almost because the few kids I did see let me know it wasn't. Our picture was taken on all the roller coasters. I am definitely letting him keep those. I felt

happiness in my heart. Once it became
nightfall with all the lights everywhere it
was magical.

Are you ready to go, Blu?

No! I hate to leave.

I feel the same way but we need to beat the
crowd out of here.

 "Thank you, I had such a great time. My
teddy bear is so cute. I got all this stuff
like a little kid, but I'm not complaining,
because these things will keep me reminded
of the best time I had today."

"I'm glad you enjoyed yourself, sweetie. You
need to get anything from the store before I
take you home?"

"No thank you, I'm good." While we riding
I'm thinking to myself, Why do I have an ill
feeling in my stomach? I got butterflies and
shit. Just feeling weird.

"You okay?"

"Yeah, just tired. I'm going in and go to bed after my bath."

"Well, I got you home, safe and sound. Can I have a hug?"

"Sure, and thank you so much, Brent." Next thing you know I was kissing him, leaving him no choice but to kiss me. Damn! Here go that ill ass feeling again, Anyway! Whatever!

"Can I talk to you tomorrow?" Brent, you can call me whenever you want to talk.

"Drive safe."

No sooner than I stepped under the car-porch, Thad jumped out from behind the house.

"Where the fuck you been?"

I was scared and very jumpy because he had a
look like he wanted to get violent and hit
me or something. "I went out!"

"Out where?"

"I really don't feel like getting into this
with you. I'm tired, and what are you doing
here anyway?" The moment had arrived. Thad
slapped me so hard my head hit the bricks on
the car-porch wall. My ears started ringing
and my face instantly burned. I tried to be
strong and hold back the tears and show no
emotion. I started walking off and he
slapped me again. I don't know why I didn't
fight back, just stood there while tears
filled my eyes.

"You ain't nothing but a lil Hoe! You a
dirty sneaky lil Bitch!"

I turned toward the door praying he wouldn't
stop me. I open the door, he didn't follow

me so no one could see him. I walked in as if nothing was wrong. Damn! Granma sitting right on the couch.

"You had a good time, sweetheart?"
"Yeah, the best." I walked straight ahead without stopping to my room. I didn't look her way so she wouldn't notice anything. I didn't even take a bath. I laid across the bed and fell asleep with my clothes on.

The sun is really bright this morning. I went into the bathroom to wash my face and take a shower. Oh My God! My eye is bloodshot red and my face is swollen. What am I going to do? I can't let Granma or anybody see me. I can't believe two slaps to the face cause this kind of damage.

"Lord Have Mercy! What happen to you?" Granma asked.

"Oh, while I was at Six Flags I got hit across the face with one of the safety bars getting off a ride."

"Okay, well you need some ice and some eye drops for that eye. It looks like a busted blood vessel in your eye."

"I'll be all right. I'm just staying inside until it heals."

"Good idea, because that's a mess."

I put on a pajama short set after I showered and got in my bed and waited for Granma to get back from the drugstore with the eye drops. This is, I know, about the tenth time this phone has rung. It's nobody but Thad. Why is he calling?

"Hello?"

"I been calling all morning. I wanted to speak to you before I come over."

"You didn't speak to me before you came over last night, and we don't have nothing to talk about. Goodbye." I layed there and went to sleep after I turned off my ringer. Thad woke me up shaking my leg.

"Blu, please talk to me, baby. I'm so sorry. What you want me to do? I'll do anything it's me and you."

Well, that's typical. I guess that's what's supposed to be said after a person hits somebody. It sounds like a bunch of bullshit to me.

"I'm not letting you go, Blu. It's me and you. No other way, you hear me?"

"Yeah, I hear you, but that sounds like a threat." In my mind, I'm scared of him and this situation and don't even understand this fear. Instead of thinking of a way to be free from him, I started thinking of a

way to make the best of this. I felt stuck.
I didn't know what to do. Time has gone by
and I've been going through the motions with
Thad. He hasn't been horrible but still
trying to control everything about me. As
the events that are affecting me right now
keeps unfolding, I'm going to try to get
through my troubles and find a way to tell
Thad that I'm pregnant and I have found the
perfect apartment after looking at several.

Chapter Three

"**Blu, why did** we get a two-bedroom when we could have gotten a one-bedroom?"

"Well, Thadius Glover, you about to be a daddy in a few months, and we're going to need the room."

"I knew it. I knew you were looking funny, acting strange and gaining weight, too!"

"I have a OB appointment tomorrow. I'm going to catch the bus and stop at the mall of georgia, go to the cookie shop and browse around at the baby store. I'll be back before it gets dark since I'll be on the bus."

"Why the bus? I mean, we do have a car."

"I know, I want to make a little day of it and get some exercise at the same time."

"What are you up to, girl? Who you trying to get with?"

"You can't be serious. HELLO!!! I'm pregnant and just going to the doctor. What's the problem, Thad? I need to get out, that's all. You have isolated me from my family. I don't talk to anybody. I haven't seen my Granma in months. I haven't talk to my mom since I don't know when. I have no friends and I'm miserable."

"Yeah, Whatever! I'm taking you to the doctor tomorrow."

"But you have to work!"

"Don't worry about what I have to do."

I just turned over and thought about how trapped I felt and how much my true feelings hated him. He did practically whatever he wanted, and I was confined to the apartment.

The months went by and Thad came and went
while I stayed stuck in the apartment.

"Thadius, you are always gone and I'm here
with no phone. What if something happens?"

"Like what?"

"Anything could happen."

"You are okay, so let that go, girl."

"Where you about to go?"

"Over to see my buddy and watch the game."

"Drop me at my granma's . I haven't seen her
in I don't know how long." But he just
walked out the door and locked it as if I'd
said nothing. I was so mad. I sat on the
floor and put a puzzle together. Halfway
through the puzzle being completed my body
start feeling funny. I just didn't feel
good. I got a cushion from the sofa and lay
there. My water broke. I panic so I sat on
the toilet at first then put on a maxi-pad

to try and control the water. I'm feeling so much pressure so I put my hand between my legs and held it there while I walk to the neighbor's apartment.

"Hi, can you help me? My water broke and I need to use your phone to call for help." The man scream to the back of the house and a lady ran out and said, "Come in, honey, and lie on the sofa."

"No thanks, I just need to use your phone." I called 911 and went back to my apartment and waited on my ride to the hospital. I'm sitting here in this quiet apartment alone. I'm not afraid yet but my body is tingling all over. I feel abandoned and like I'm in this world alone, just like before. Thad actually can be here this time but he's not. I was thinking about how I want my baby to be healthy so I tried to think of something pleasant. It felt like somebody said, "Lights, Camera, Action!" I never seen so many doctors, nurses and a whole lot more people make such a fuss over me. When I was getting checked in the emergency room, I heard somebody say, "She's already ten centimeters. Okay, Ms. Spencer, you need to push when I count to three." We did that about five times. "Here comes the baby," someone said.

It's a girl! I can't believe I'm not in that much pain. It feels like a dull menstrual cramp. "Can I hold my baby?"

"Yes, you sure can. As a matter of fact, you can hold both of them in a few minutes."

"WHAT?"

"I need you to push, Ms. Spencer. On the count of three, just like the first time." I pushed about ten times on this one. It's another girl.

"Let the nurses get them ready and you can hold them." Oh my god. I got two babies.

"Ms. Spencer, you have identical twins. One is five pounds, and the other is five pounds ten ounces." Wow, they so small. One has all these curls of hair and the other is bald.

"Well, now you have to buy another set of clothes," the nurse said.

"Yes, I know." I already didn't have a baby shower, and now I've just got the surprise of my life. TWINS! I was thinking, Lord you must have some plans for me. I started feeling like God gave me two babies because of the situation with my first pregnancy. I was overjoyed and overwhelmed at the same time.

"Baby, I'm so sorry I wasn't there for the birth of our baby. Excuse me, babies. How you feeling?"

"I'm okay, just tired and hungry."

"Pardon me, I need to get your vitals and then take the babies to the nursery so we can complete a few more things with them. They'll be back in a couple of hours."

"So Ms. Spenser, what's their names?"

"I'm going to go with Sky Marie and Zoey Marie."

"Being the dad, I guess I have no say so in that?"

"Nope! Cause when I first laid eyes on them those names came to mind instantly. Thad, who told you I was here?"

"Somebody put a note on the door saying where you are."

"Oh, that was the people who phone I used. We have to get a phone and more things for these babies. The hospital say they will give me packages of everything I need for them to last me at least three months." The nurse took the babies. Me and Thad sat in silence for a while. "I need to call my family and let them know I had the babies. Everybody gone be so shock to know that it's two babies."

"Blu, why didn't we know it was two?"

"Because we never saw the baby on the ultrasound or heard a different heartbeat. It doesn't matter. God bless me with two. Period. Anyway, call my Granma. You already know she think she's too young and sexy to be a great-granma." She's straight up

Italian with an attitude. Granma thinks that wearing her hair in that bun on top of her head with those baby doll curls on the side makes her look young. She tall and very shapely for her age. She is around 70 years old, and still wear heels, not to mention still having sex. I'm young and I don't have the kind of energy she has sometimes.

"Thad, will you please call her?"

"Blu, can we have this moment to ourselves for a while? We will get with your family later." See, here he go! It never fails. I'm thinking to myself I will call when he leave after visiting hours.

"Hello!"

"Is this you, Granma?"

"Yes, is this Blu?"

"Yeah, it's me!"

"Well, how you doing, sweetheart?"

"I'm okay. I'm in the hospital. I just had twins."

"Oh My Goodness! I wanna know all about them. I'll call Cora and we will come see you tomorrow. What do you need?"

"Granma, I need everything, because the second baby was a complete surprise."

"Where's that Thadius?"

"He's gone home. They let the father stay overnight, but I kept quiet about that because I was not feeling it. Well, Granma, I will see y'all tomorrow. Come anytime between visiting hours. I will be here! I love you, Granma."

"I love you, too, sweetheart. Bye bye."

"I don't eat oatmeal. Do you have anything else for breakfast? I'll have some toast and bacon if possible."

"I'll see what I can do after I deliver the rest of the trays."

"Okay, thanks! I'm hungry as hell this morning after having those babies."

"Hi there, new mommy."

"Hey mamma, where Granma?"

"Out there at the nursery window. Girl, your Granma has bought these babies everything from Baby Gap, Wal-Mart and Kids-R-Us. Thad called this morning, so we dropping everything by your apartment, when we leave. Then I guess he will head down here after that."

"What did he say when he called?"

"He let us know about the babies, their names, how much they weighed, and you know, just the whole rundown. But your Granma already knew that from your phone call last night."

"I can't believe he called. That was nice of him." Cora and Granma stayed for a while, then said they'd come see us when we got home. "The doctor said I can go home tomorrow." I didn't see Thad until it was time to go on that third day. He never came after Granma and Mamma left.

Chapter Four

I talked to my dad the day I got ready to leave the hospital. He had been sick again. He didn't sound good on the phone, but he perked up a little when he heard he had twin grand girls. The fire department gave us two car seats. Over the next year Thad became even more controlling and possessive. I still couldn't go anywhere without asking permission. A couple of friends from high school talk with Granma to find out where I was and start coming by from time to time. Thad would say they wanted him or they would say how mean and rude he was, so they stopped visiting after a while. I would ask to use the car to just go to the mall, visit Granma or whatever. He would always ask what was in it for him. "What's in it for me to let you use the car?" he would say. Bottom line: "I want you to give me head or let me hit that thang in the back." I can honestly say at this point I despise this man.

A lot of times, after I put the girls to bed he would take all my clothes out of the closet, including the ones I had on and put them in the trunk of his black Range Rover with chrome rims, windows lightly tinted, not too much. He had it looking very nice, and he look nice in it. During the day, while Thad was at work I would be home with only a slip on. If he came home and I had on something of his he would snatch it off and torture me. He came home Friday evening. I'm so used to him not showing up until the a.m. hours, I forgot to take his shorts and t-shirt off. I was laying across the bed. The girls were taking a late nap from playing all day. "Blu, what do you have on?" Before

I could answer he put the pillow over my face until I stopped fighting him to get it off. He started bending all my fingers back, popping off nails that I got when I went to the grocery store.

"Stop it, Thadius!" My fingers are bleeding. He then started choking me until I was seeing blue dots. "Please stop!"

"I'll stop if you can tell me you have learned your lesson. When I say no clothes, that's what I mean. Now go wash your hands and clean up these nails and shit. Put some gloves on when you cook. Your fingers are bleeding and I don't want that crap in my food." I went in the bathroom thinking to myself, *Why the hell is he here? He comes here just to have sex with me and torture me.*

It's Saturday morning. Thad got up and left. He took the twins with him. I guess they were going to his parents' house. I'm here watching *The Bridges of Madison County* with Meryl Streep and Clint Eastwood. *Who could be at my door?*

"Who is it?"

"It's your neighbor, Blu!"

"Oh, hey Sandy. How's it going?"

"I'm doing fine. I saw Thad and the kids leave, so I ran on over here. Do you have a phone yet?"

"No."

"Oh, okay, I have a cell phone in this box that you can have if you want it."

"Yes, I want it! Thank you. I just got to keep it hid from you-know-who."

"Yeah, well, it's yours, and all the information about it is in the box. I'll come back by on Monday after he leaves for work."

"Okay, talk to you later."

Sandy was about 300 pounds and she is the nicest person I've ever met, and she can sew her ass off. Sandy and her man are the ones whose phone I used when my water broke with the girls. Our friendship has been undercover, but we are very close. Sandy has dark skin with real deep dimples. Her hair is styled in a short bob and she always wear long skirts and buttoned-down blouses with slits on each side. I set the phone up with all the numbers I know and charged it up. I call my dad before I turned the phone off and hid it. A lady answered the phone.

"I'm not sure if I have the right number, but may I speak to Lawrence Spencer?"

"Yes, you have the right number. I'm a nurse at the hospital. Mr. Spencer asked if we could answer his phone to inform people that he has been admitted."

"Hey Daddy, how you feeling? The nurse gave me your room number."

"Hey there, little girl, how you doing?"

"Oh, I'm okay. I just call to check on you, not knowing you in the hospital again. I know those nurses love waiting on you."

"Yeah, I can't keep them out of this room."

"Well, Daddy, you a good looking brother. It's always been said that women love a tall, dark, handsome man."

"I guess that's what your mama loved. How is your mom?"

"I'm sure she's good, but I'm worried about you, Dad."

"The doctor said I can probably go home in a few days and I'm gone be just fine. I have to stop drinking, though. My ankles are swollen again so I have to take it easy."

"Yes, you do."

"I got a little while left in me girl, so I can see those little dolls I got for granddaughters."

"Even though the girls are identical, I see all of us in them, Daddy."

"I show the girls' pictures to everybody. Blu, they look just like you and Cora to me. I keep the pictures in my wallet so they with me all the time. I love showing off my grandbabies. Where is Sky and Zoey's sperm donor?"

"His name is Thad!"

"I know that boy name. I just chose not to say it. Blu, I don't like him. It's just something about him. And you so damn secretive when it comes to him."

"Anyway, Daddy, you just concentrate on getting well and I will try to come see you tomorrow."

"No, don't come. Call me instead, because I prefer to see you guys when I'm out on my feet."

"Okay, I love you, Mr. Billy-Dee Williams look-alike!"

"Uh-huh, me too."

Now, where can I hide this phone? Perfect!
I'll keep it in the bottom of my tampon box.

Chapter Five

Thad brought the girls home Saturday night around 9 p.m., showered, put on clothes, and said he'd be back later. Don't wait up. The girls and I just watched movies for the rest of the weekend. Here it is Monday. Is he dead? Did he move out? What in the hell is going on? I just heard a car door. Now I hear Thad coming in the front door, moving all fast.

"What's up, Blu? I'm late for work, so I'll talk to you and tell you what happen to me when I get home this evening."

I laid there as if I was still asleep. After Thad left in a hurry and lock the door behind him I got up. Between the psychological scarring and emotional pain, I can't seem to get my thoughts together and figure out what to do. I do know I can't just be like a hostage in this apartment. Sky and Zoey will be starting school soon, and something has to give. Reality has been in the air all day. I could almost smell it and I definitely saw it for the first time. Thad was keeping the bills paid for the sake of his daughters.

"Today has been a long day! What you and the twins been doing all day?"

"No! Don't you think you may wanna tell me why you left here on Saturday and returned on Monday?"

"Girl, you don't want for nothing! And anyway, I was out trying to put a game plan together with a partner of mine. We about to start making some real money." He makes descent money at Clorox Distribution and he's been there a few years. Thad will always have that hustle in his blood. He dabbled in selling dope coming out of high school and never stopped, I guess.

"So that's your answer, Thad?"

"I just told you what was up, Blu. Oh, Did FedEx deliver a package Saturday?"

"No, it came today. Why were all these clothes delivered for the twins?"

"Blu, just accept the shit and don't worry about where it came from."

Me and my migraine headache just walked into the kitchen and sat at the table.

"Why you in there sitting at the table? Come get in the bed."

"Huh?"

"You heard me, girl. Come get in the bed."

"Oh, I'm not tired."

"Good, that means you can go for a ride."

"You think so?"

"I know so, Blu. Besides, you don't have a choice."

I reluctantly rode his unprotected, been-out-in-the-street, possibly sick dick. After Thad had done nothing through this fifteen-minute sexcapade he was still breathing harder than a dragon. I told him I need to take him to work tomorrow so I can use the car.

"What do you need the car for?"

"I need to go food shopping, along with getting toiletries and things."

"Blu, you can do that when I get home."

"I want to get out this house, too."

"Aight! But don't go left on me, girl." I wonder to myself what the hell he's talking about. I turned over and squeezed my eyes shut until I fell asleep.

I'm glad his ass is out of the car and at work. Now I can ride peacefully, handle my business real quick and then go to the mall or something.

"Oh, yes honey! That dress is sharp as hell on you."

"You think so?"

"Hell yes. You need to get that."

"Well I'm just looking, I ain't buying." This chick is standing behind me while I'm in this boutique trying on clothes. The twins running around the store like they just got let out of a cage. The lady standing behind me is about 5'6 and one hundred twenty five pounds. She has a cute, honey-blonde, short, tapered haircut and brown eyes. She has on a long t-shirt with some leggings and sandals. Plain but cute.

Her coach bag on her arm looks like a overnight bag that's the same color as her sandals. She's brown skin and very friendly.

"Girl, are those your twins?"

"Yes, and they kind of crunk up right now. I'm Blu. What's your name?"

"Starsha, but everybody call me Starr. Blu, you are so pretty, and your girls are adorable!"

"Thank you!"

"I have five boys, so you know I love little girls."

"Wow! Five boys, huh! Well, it was nice to meet you Starr. Take care. Zoey and Sky, let's go."

"Girls, please sit still and put your seatbelts on." I started up the car and Starr scared me by knocking on my window.

"Hey, Blu. You look like you like to relax on a occasional glass of wine. Girl, let me get your number!"

"I tell you what, Starr. Let me get your number and I'll give you a call before the week is over and we can plan something for next weekend."

"Okay, Blu, sounds good." I pulled off feeling annoyed because I can't even give out a telephone number. Not to mention the fact that I have to sneak and call Starr so it won't be known in my house that I have a phone. I'm on my way to get Thad and the closer I get, my thoughts, feelings, everything just change for the worse.

After picking Thad up from work, we got home and settled in for the evening. "Where you fixin' to go?"

"I told you before that me and some buddies trying to get some business kicked off. I won't be out long, I promise." I just walked out the room and went to look in on the girls. I knew it would be pointless to say anything, so I said nothing. Once I heard that all-too-familiar sound of him closing and locking the door behind him, I got my phone out of the tampon box and called my dad.

Chapter Six

I figured he would be out the hospital by
now. The voicemail has come on all three
times I called. Not knowing if Dad is still
in the hospital or not, I tried his hospital
room number. "This is room one eleven, may I
help you?"

"Yes! Is this Lawrence Spencer's room?"

"Yes, it is. I'm the hospice nurse assigned
to Mr. Spencer. Who am I speaking with?"

"Did you say hospice?"

"Yes, but who am I speaking with?"

"I'm his daughter! Why are you there with my
dad?"

"Mr. Spencer has to get his hospice care
here at the hospital because he has no next
of kin and no permanent address."

"What are you saying? I'm his next of kin. I'm his daughter!"

"Okay, but there is nothing documented anywhere about you or any other family member."

"Put my dad on the phone, please."

"What is your name?"

"Blu Spenser is my name. Please put my dad on the phone!"

"I'm sorry, but he's unable to communicate on the phone. Ms. Spenser, maybe it would be a good idea if you come to the hospital and you can learn more about your father's condition."

I just hung up on the nurse, don't really know why because she hasn't done anything wrong. I'm thinking that I just need to sit with myself for a minute and regroup. What is Daddy's condition? I have to get to that hospital. I'm going first thing in the morning when Thad go to work. Wait! What am I saying? I'm gonna get the car tomorrow and go see my dad.

I fix dinner as usual, but can't eat. I lay down instead. I don't know when Thad came in because he never made it past the sofa. The alarm clock woke me up because it's automatically set to get him up in the morning.

"Thadius, I need to take you to work!"

"Why?"

"I have to go see my dad. He is in the hospital."

"And how do you know that?" He is continuing to get dressed, and asks again in a dry tone. "How do you know your dad is in the hospital?"

"I called him and a nurse is taking his calls."

"Who phone did you use?"

"That is so not important right now. I just need the car."

"I'm waiting on you to tell me, who phone you used."

"Fuck it! And fuck you!" Did I just say that? Ooh, I'm tripping! I got the girls and walk to that bus stop a mile away. I don't know what time it comes, I'll just wait on it. Thadius rode right past us. The bus is on time, here before we even get to the bus stop. The girls and I rode straight into town and walked to the hospital.

My dad was on the first floor, room one eleven. I walked in and the nurse asked my name.

"I'm his daughter, Blu Spencer."

"Ms. Spencer, I'm so sorry for your loss." I sat down in the chair near the door to the room. My dad's bed was by the window. The curtain was pulled and I could only see his feet. I continued to sit there hoping that when I walked over to that bed it would be someone else. The girls were in the waiting area about two doors down. I asked the nurse if she would walk over with me. "How long has he been gone?"

"Oh, he passed about thirty minutes before you got here." All I could think about was that if I had driven the car I would have been here.

Wow, his body is still so warm. I sat with him for what seemed like forever. I think an hour or so went by, and some people came in and said they have to take him. The tears just won't come right now. I feel numb. I went to the nurses' station and called Granma. "Blu, let me call your mamma. You stay right there. We coming to get you."

"The girls and I will wait in the cafeteria because they need to eat."

The girls screamed when they saw her, "Gigi, Gigi, we wanna go with you!" That's short for great-granma.

"Granma, where is Mamma?"

"You know your mamma, Blu, she said she can't handle this kind of stuff."

"This is not about her. Anyway, the hospital wants to know who to release Daddy to and so on."

Granma Lena said, "I'll handle everything. You just go home and I will see you in a couple of days."

"Can you drop me and the girls off at home, Now?"

"Sure I can."

On the way home I'm thinking, *Damn. I don't know what's gonna go down at my house between me and Thad, considering how I left this morning.*

"Listen, girls. Mommy is very tired. I need y'all to make some peanut butter and jelly sandwiches. Get your juices and chips or whatever. Clean up your areas on the table, and then go in your room and put a movie on. Wash up first and put on your nightclothes, okay? Be little big girls and help me, okay?" They will be ten years old on their next birthday.

Zoey is the outspoken one, so she always speaks on behalf of both of them. Sky should have been named Shy, because that's what she is. I laid across my bed with this migraine. I took some pain pills and continued to lay there.

"What's up, Blu?" I still lay there in silence because for the first time all day I felt extremely sad and just wanted to cry. "What's wrong with you? And why my girls in the bed? And why it's so dark in here?"

"My dad passed away this morning, and I would appreciate it if you would leave me the hell alone!" Thad just stood there for a second then walked in the kitchen and got a beer. He never returned to the bedroom. I stayed in bed the next day and the next day and maybe even the one after that. Thad took our girls with him the next morning. I'm assuming to his parents.

Finally, Granma came by. "Blu, it's going to be a small service at the chapel. I will pick you up tomorrow morning around nine. I ask no questions. I just went along with everything until my dad was laid to rest. Yesterday was hard as hell burying my dad.

Chapter Seven

I'm not in love with Thad, although I do have love for him, considering we have been together for a long time and share children. The girls have been gone for a week. I've just been home thinking and reflecting on everything in my world. I'm just lying here and for some reason Starr popped in my mind.

"Hi, may I speak to Starr?"

"This is she. Who is this?"

"My name is Blu. We met at the dress shop."

"Oh, hey Blu! Damn, girl, loosen up. Don't be so formal. I thought you weren't going call me."

"I would have called you already, but my dad passed away, among other things."

"Oh, I'm sorry about your dad. This means we have to hurry and hook up so you can feel better about everything, whatever it may be."

"Sounds good to me, Starr. I need everything to be good in my life right now."

"Well, Blu, your new BFF is here, girl. I'm putting some things together and I will call you back, Ms. Blu. Blu. Hmmmm, what an intriguing name."

"But Starr, you don't have my number."

"It's on my caller ID."

"Oh, okay, well talk to you later."

For the first time, I put my phone in my purse and not in the tampon box. I got up and walk to Sandy's house.

"Hell is about to freeze over! Blu, you haven't been over here since you had those babies."

"I know, girl. What's up?"

"Nothing, come in, please."

"Just came to sit with my best friend. Is that okay with you Sandy? Cause you always come to my house."

"I don't mind, because I know your situation."

"Thank you for understanding without judging."

"Well, I'm your friend. I'm here to support you and be there when I can. Blu, we have become very close and you will always be my sister."

"Thank you, Sandy, I really appreciate that."

"Would you like a drink?"

"Now, Sandy, you know I don't really drink."

"Is it that you don't drink, or you haven't
had an opportunity to drink?"

I laughed and said, "Girl, pour the drink,
and don't forget the chaser."

"You want Coke as your chaser for this
Hennessy?"

"No, ma'am! Ice is the chaser I need."

"One Hennessy on the rocks coming up for Ms.
Blu." Sandy and I drank, laugh, talk, and
then ate some wings. Drank, laugh, talk and
ate some more, until we were full and drunk
as hell.

"I'ma take it on in, because my head is
spinning and I need to lay down."

"Okay, Blu. I'll holla at you tomorrow."

"Where the fuck you been, Blu?"

"Oh, I didn't think you would be home."

"And? What does that mean? Girl, you gone make me..."

Before Thad could finish his sentence I said, "I'm not about to let you ruin my night with your bullshit. You might as well climb into bed and call it a night like I'm about to do." I woke up with Thad on top of me trying to force his way inside.

"What's wrong with you? Why you so dry?"

"I don't want to do this right now, I'm sick!"

"You ain't sick!" He forced his way in. I just laid there and let my mind take me somewhere else, after wishing he would die instantly.

The next morning I told Thad to get the twins because I need to see my babies.

"My parents took them to the country. They will be back tomorrow."

I went and ran me some bathwater, hot as possible. I was sitting in the tub, thinking and crying. I don't want to stay here, but I have nowhere to go. Good, I heard him leave. Nasty dog, didn't even bathe before he left. That's unlike him, but whatever. After I get dressed I guess I'll call Starr and tell her I need to take her up on that drink.

"What's good, Starr? It's Blu! What's on your agenda for today?"

"Hold on a minute, Blu...Who is it?" Whoever was at her door apparently was supposed to come last night. I could hear her saying, "What happened to you? Well, we were supposed to get it done last night, but I guess we can do it today...Hello, sorry about that, girl. So, what's up?"

"Not too much. I was calling to see if you would like to do lunch and have that drink a little later."

"Let me get back to you in a couple of hours. I'm sure we can, but my guy friend just got here and we need to handle something. Oh, but I'm sure we can have that long overdue drink."

"Okay, Starr. Talk to you in a minute."

Chapter Eight

I didn't want Starr coming to my house.
I've got and have had too many problems. I
had to catch the train to NorthSprings
station. She lived a good ways from me. I
live on one side of Atlanta and she lived on
the other.

"Starr! I'm here at the station."

"Okay. Stand on the side where the buses
pull in and I will be there in five
minutes." I could have walked to your place.
You two minutes away.

"Wow! You have a really nice place. Are
these condos?"

 Yeah and very expensive.

"I know that scent—"I am King" by P. Diddy.
My girls dad wears it faithfully."

"Yeah, my guy friend just left, after his shower. I guess he bathe in the cologne, because it's kind of loud, ain't it?"

"Why do you call him your guy friend?"

"First of all, because that's what he is, and second of all, it's a small world. He's got obligations somewhere else, and so do I. You feel me?"

"Is he married?"

"Damn, Blu. Who works for the FBI? What's with all the questions?"

"Sorry, I hope I didn't step on your toes."

"No, it's not that. It's just nobody has ever asked questions about us. So Blu, where's your man?"

"In the street somewhere."

"Do you live together?"

"You can say that."

"What?"

"Oh, he's never there. I think he been fooling around for years. I never caught him, but that's mainly because I'm not looking and don't give a damn."

"Does he take care of you and the girls?"

"He pay the bills, if that's what you asking. And he use my body for sex, but there is nothing between us. Please, honey. I came here for lunch and drinks, not a psychiatrist session. Because that's what I need for that conversation!"

"Blu, I must say, you are a very pretty woman. And girl, you got a shape to die for. I don't know what your man in the streets doing, but he has a Dime at home!"

"Thanks for the compliment."

"I'm Starr, and everybody knows I call it like I see it. I don't know how you wore those heels over here on the train, but you looking so cute, so let's go out instead of staying stuck in here."

"Starr, you are gorgeous, too, so let's go!"

"What about the Cheesecake Factory?"

"Sounds good." I only had forty dollars and a breeze card paid up for the week. We ordered steak, seafood, drinks and dessert. Our tab came up to $218.00. How the hell that happen?

Starr said, "I don't know how much money you have, but I don't care, because your BFF got this. Now let's go back to my place so we can sober up. Blu, I can't get over how pretty you are. You need to be modeling or something. How tall are you?"

"I'm 5'10". So, Starr, what kind of work do you do?"

"I'm in real estate."

"It must be exciting being independent, doing your own thing. I have never had a job. I've been with one guy and had two babies. The end!"

"I need another drink. You want one?"

"Starr, I am still nice from our drinks at the restaurant."

"Come on, Blu. Have another one. I'll take you home."

"Okay, just one drink, then I have to be going. You can just take me downtown and I'll go from there." Starr poured some wine and we clinked glasses. "To friendship," we both said. Starr took me to Peachtree train station from the restaurant. Walking toward my apartment brought on depression and sadness.

The thought of being back home broke me down. I started thinking about how I was going to make some changes in my life.

"What brings you in so early tonight, Mr. Glover?"

"I'm tired. And I need to talk to you." I'm thinking to myself, *what in the hell does Thad need to talk to me about?* He has been doing his own thing for a long time. Thad is very abusive mentally and physically, and I never once have questioned him about anything because my heart began to harden the night he busted the blood vessel In my eye. "What do you want to talk about?"

"Us, that's what."

"Well, I'm listening."

"Blu, you already know I'm not the type to beat around the bush. So, I think we should get married." (*What the hell is he going through?*)

"Are you high or something?"

"No, girl! I'm serious about this. So, what do you think about it?"

"I really don't know what to think, and I sure as hell don't know what to say. Wait. Yes, I do know what to say. Thadius, with the way we live, you want to go from that into a marriage?" "There is no way in hell I will marry this nut." I'm thinking of how I can leave his ass and start living my life. I've wasted enough time doing nothing. *Hell no* is my answer, but I can't let him know that just yet.

"Let me just do some thinking, and we will talk about it later."

"Yeah, Whatever Blu. You ain't got to let me know a damn thing later. Cancel that shit. I'll be back later." And he left, mad as hell, slamming the door so hard it knocked a painting off the wall.

Chapter Nine

Now, who could be at the door at six in the morning?

"It's Mrs. Glover and the girls, Blu!"

"Oh, Hi everybody. What y'all doing here so early?"

"Hey Mommy, we got new dolls and they do everything just like real babies!"

"I see! They so pretty. Now, go put them in your room and put your things away."

"Where is Thadius?"

"I thought he was here in the front room when I came to open the door, but I see he's not. I guess he never came back from last night."

"Oh really?" Mrs. Glover had a very concerned look on her face, but didn't comment. "I would have called you, Blu, but you don't have a phone.

"I do now! Let me put my number in your phone."

"That's real good, Blu, because when I have the girls they be wanting to call you. They always saying, 'Nanna, let's call Mommy!' Well, I have to run, and I pray my son is all right."

That Negro all right, just laid up somewhere. "Yeah, I'm sure he's fine, Mrs. Glover. Drive safe, and I'll talk to you soon." I don't even believe how this motherfucker didn't come home last night. I looked at myself in the bathroom mirror. *Girl, please! You know damn well this is nothing new.* The only thing new is that I'm tired of it and ready to make some changes.

This man coming in the door going straight in the fridge like he been here all night.

"When did the girls get here?"

"It's 10 am, and if you were here you would have known the answer to that question." He just paused for a minute as though he was thinking about something he just remembered. "Thadius, what are you doing?"

"Seems to me you need a little help shutting that smart ass mouth of yours."

"No! Stop, Please!"

"Let go of the hanger, girl."

"Oh My God, what are you trying to do to me?" After he snatched a hanger from the closet, I felt the hanger dig into my throat.

"Maybe if I rip them vocal cords out then you will keep this smartass trap shut. Now Bitch, lay there and choke on your own blood." I can't hardly breathe. I can't speak. I see Zoey standing there, but where is Sky? I wanna call out to her but I can't I want to say "Don't be scared, Zoey," but I can't say anything.

"Mommy, Sky is in the kitchen with Daddy." Oh My God, he is still here. What do I do? *Save me, Lord,* is all I can say to myself. I see his shadow on the wall. I'm trying to sit up but I can't. Both girls are standing there screaming, "No Daddy!" I can see a knife in his hand. He grab my hair and wrapped it around his fist and just cut it off. I felt the knife cut me, and it feels like some warm water on the side of my head. Just for a second there was no pain, but now it's stinging. I was about to grab my ear when I caught Thad's fist on my cheek. *Where are my girls?* I can't see or hear anything. If I can just get to my purse and get my phone. I wonder if Thad is still in the house. *Where is my purse? Where are the girls?* These same questions keep coming in my head over and over again. I can't understand why he would take a wire hanger and open my mouth, stabbing me in my throat with it, then just beat on me. Why? Not to mention cut my hair off with a knife. I just want to know, why? All I can do is lie here and continue to ask God to save me.

"Ma'am, can you hear me?"

"Her name is Mommy."

"Okay, sweetheart, go sit in the kitchen with the officer. "Ma'am, on three we're going to lift you up on the stretcher." I can't see anything. Who is talking to me? Questions run through my mind, but I can't speak them. "Ma'am, your daughter called for

help with a neighbor's assistance. We're
going to get you to the hospital."

Chapter Ten

"Ms. Spencer, here's a pen and paper so you can write what you want to say."

"Where are my girls? How long have I been in this hospital bed?"

"I'm the RN caring for you. My name is Lora. You've been here for six days."

I quickly scribbled again on the paper. "You mean to tell me I have been asleep for six days?"

"Well, you have been sedated. Your throat was very swollen, so we needed to intubate you for a few days in order for you to breathe. Just keep writing, Ms. Spencer. I want to answer all of your questions to the best of my ability."

"Where are my children?"

"I assume they are with family, because you've had just one visitor."

"Who?"

"Your best friend, Sandy. Your visitors have to be approved for your safety. You've been banged up a bit. It will take some time for you to heal."

"Do you know how long I will be here?"

"Once the swelling goes down in your throat enough for you to breathe and swallow on your own, then we will see. Okay?"

"Wake up, Blu, it's Sandy."

"Hello, I'm the nurse taking care of her this evening. She can mumble words, but mostly she writes what she wants to say on that notepad."

"How are you feeling, Blu?"

"I'm glad you're here, Sandy. Where are Sky and Zoey?"

"They with Ms. Lena."

"How did they get with my Granma?"

"I kept them for a few days, then I took them to her."

"Why haven't they come to see me?"

"Ms. Lena said she calls every day, and it's better if she and the girls see you when you come home."

"Have you seen Thad around our apartment?"

"I saw him once."

"The nurse said I been here six days."

"No, honey, you've been here close to thirty days now."

"WHAT!"

"Just relax, Blu, and continue to get well. The girls are fine, and you know where they are, so just concentrate on getting well."

It's been a month and a half, and I feel better. I'm glad I don't have to use that notepad to talk and I'm getting out of this hospital.

"Ms. Spencer, I've covered all the do's and don'ts. Just remember to take it easy, because you're not one hundred percent yet."
"I'm her best friend and neighbor, so I will help make sure she follow doctor's orders."

I'm happy to be out the hospital, but this car-ride has me feeling not so great. Kind of sick, like.
"Sandy, why you driving so slow?"

"Because I'm not sure if you should go to that apartment or to your Granma house."
"My Granma lives in a high-rise community for the elderly. If the apartment is still ours then I have to go there. I have nowhere

else to go."

"What about Thad, Blu?"

"What about him?"

"As your best friend, I need you to know I'm totally against this."

"Sandy, do you have somewhere for me and the girls?"

"Unfortunately, No."

"Okay then, Wheew! I'm glad we made it to the apartment. I will get the girls tomorrow." "Wow! It's so clean in here. I wonder where my purse is."

"Zoey gave it to me when we called for help."

"Sandy, your purse is too big if mine can fit inside of yours." We both laughed.

"Anyway, honey, here's your little purse. I'ma go home. I will call you later to check on you."

I lock the door like Thad don't have a key. I laid on the sofa, because I'm not ready to go in that bedroom.

"Hey Starr!"

"Blu, is that you? Where the hell you been hiding? I have called your phone at least a million times and I have left a billion messages."

"Girl, you so crazy! I been in the hospital for over a month. I really don't want to go into it, but I will say, me and my man got into it and I got hurt. So please, can we leave it there? Maybe one day we can talk about it, but not now. I need to move forward."

"Okay, Blu, if you say so, but I'm here for you."

"Yeah, I know. So, Ms. Starr, what's the business with you, personally and professionally?"

"I'm still taking it easy, doing my thing as far as work goes. And my guy friend's been under me a lot more lately."
"Well, that's a good thing, right?"

"It's okay sometimes. Speaking of that, he won't be back for a couple of days. Why don't you come over tomorrow? I can pick you up."

"I will have my friend Sandy drop me off."
"Why? Blu, I have a car and I don't mind at all. We have become good friends, and you so damn private about your house and your man."

"Starr, I don't know who your man is either, you always say 'my guy friend.'"

"Okay, Okay! Forget the guys, and let's concentrate on you coming over tomorrow. I will call you when I'm on my way."

"Oh my goodness, Blu, where is your hair?"

"It's gone."

"Hell, I see that!"

"I'll keep it pulled back until I can figure out what to do with it. My hair has always been long, and now it's just chopped off."

"Let me take you to my stylist. I only have to make a phone call."

"No, thank you!"

"Okay, let me bring someone here. Your hair is so pretty with those deep locks of curls. Come on, Blu, let me help you." The stylist texted, she will be here within the hour. Maybe a drink will help us decide what we eating after you get that Do done. Blu, get the door please. She got here quick.

"I'm Wanda. And I wasn't told you look like a porcelain doll, Gorgeous! Can I give you a major cut, like Halle Berry, maybe?"

"Yeah, I don't care."

This drink is not helping me relax as Wanda
do the finishing touches on my hair. So! How
do you like it? I'm happy with it. Thank
you!

Starr walked Wanda to the door while I stood
at the mirror admiring my hair. Very short,
but cute.

"You like seafood?"

"I love seafood. Let me get the menu out the
drawer and we can order in. This is a good
time for me to eat it girl, my guy friend
hates it."

"I don't get to eat it often myself, the
girls' dad is allergic to it. Does your guy
friend live here with you?"
"No, but he is here a lot, and even more

lately. What's going on with you and your Man?"

"Absolutely nothing, Starr, so drop it."

"Why don't you stay the night here? Let's have a mini-sleepover. Let's take our food and go in the room and watch an old movie. Blu, I got some pajamas you can sleep in."

"Girl, I haven't seen Imitation of Life in so long! Thank you, Starr, for everything."
"My pleasure, Blu."

"Where are "your" pj's?" You went in the bathroom and came out naked.
"Girl, I sleep in the nude. I can't stand clothes while I'm trying to relax."

"I'm your company and you need some clothes on. I mean, Damn. You don't even have on any panties."
"We got the same thing, Blu. What's the

problem?"

"You are spoiling me over here. I'm never going home. I have never had breakfast in bed."

"Blu, you have been through a lot. I want to know every detail, but you will talk when you ready. Whenever that day come, know that your girl, Starr, is a good listener."

"I'll remember that."

"I ran you a bubble bath, too."

"You didn't have to do that." What is this girl doing? Is she truly this nice, or is this some kind of bullshit I need to be concerned about?

"Move over, Blu. This Jacuzzi is big enough for both of us."

"Huh? I thought you ran this bath for me."

"I did, just close your eyes and let the jets and bubbles take effect." Starr began to massage my feet. I said nothing. She moved up my thigh.

"Wait!"

"There is nothing wrong with me helping you relax, is there? Blu, let me explain something to you. I know you straight, and so am I. We both got men in our lives. I want you to explore and you will be surprised at how good you will feel."
"I'm not comfortable with you touching me, Starr."

"Okay, let me show you something real quick and you be honest about the way you feel, okay?" My eyes are closed and this girl is massaging me and sucking on my breast at the same time.

"Stop! That's enough! I'm not gay, Starr."

"Neither am I, Blu. I'm just being there for you in every way I can."

"I love our friendship, but let's not do this because it's going to ruin it."

"All right, but don't leave. I have to go to the mall. Will you go with me? I'm going to get my guy friend's kids some things."

"Okay, but I'm not shopping with you, I'll get Sandy to get me from the mall. Do you spend time with your friend's kids?"

"No, I shop for him because he don't have time. He has two daughters, but I've never met them."

"Really? Well, my twins' dad buys for them all the time. He does a lot of shopping for them to be a man. I must say, he does well. He always buys nice things."

Chapter Eleven

"**Thank you for** picking me up, Sandy."

"You know, Thad was home when I left to come get you."

Seems like I blinked my eyes and we were home already. Talk to you later, Sandy.

"What's up, Blu?" I threw my hand up and went into the bedroom for the first time. Snapshots of what happened keep popping into my head. I feel sick to my stomach. I can't see how he just sitting in the front room like none of this ever happened. Why isn't he in jail? Am I supposed to go press charges? I know the answer to these questions, but I let them remain in my head.

"For what it's worth, I'm so sorry for what happened. Are you listening?" I kept my back turned and said nothing. "You look so pretty with your hair cut like that." He Trippin! Why is he even commenting on my hair, considering he chopped it off with a butcher knife? "If you need or want anything, just ask and it's yours." I wish he'd die. Why is he talking to me?

Who could be calling me? "Hello there, Blu, how you doing?"

"I'm okay, Mrs. Glover."

"I called because I want to have the girls come stay with me. I'm so sorry you going through a storm right now. I can keep the twins until things settle down."

"Your son hurt me bad. I'm not sure if he was trying to kill me or what, but I wouldn't hardly call any of it a storm."

"I don't approve of what he did to you, and I let him know it. You have to decide what you want to do about you and him. Nobody else can do that. I'm your children's grandmother, but as a woman and a friend, I do know you need time to heal mentally and physically. I will get the girls and when you get your strength back then come get your babies."

"They at my granma's house."

"I will give her a call if you will give me the number so I can pick them up."

"Thank you, Mrs. Glover."

 My bathtub, my pajamas, my bed with clean linen is all I need right now. I heard Thad leave while I was on the phone.

As usual, Thad is walking back in the door the next day.

"What's up? I got Sky and Zoey a couple of outfits. You want to see them?"

"I'll see later. Just put the bags in their room. Why do you always get one size bigger than the other? You know they are the same size."

"A lot of times boosters get this stuff, so they can't get the same size. Pin the clothes that's too big." I ignore his explanation. It's easier to do that now.

I miss my children. I want to go get them from Mrs. Glover, even though she just got them from my granma. I know I need to use this time to get myself together like she suggested. I think Starr got the message that we need to stay platonic friends without the "Extra Love" she trying to give me. She seems to know a lot of people. I'm going to talk to her about me working, getting a job somewhere doing something. I think she'd be happy to connect me. Thadius sitting in here watching TV. "I can see very well what you doing, Blu. I want to talk to you. Is that okay?"

"Yeah, that's okay." I'm afraid to say "Eat shit and die, motherfucker and talk to Lucifer when you get to hell," because last time he came to me in a talking mood I ended up half dead in the hospital. "I said it's okay. What's up, Thad?"

"Do you hate me, Blu?"

"I wanna blame it on the children and say that's why I don't hate you, but honestly I think I'm a woman who won't claim hate. I would appreciate it if we could leave that subject right there."

"I can respect that. I can also read between the lines, so I will leave it there."

"Well, Thad, can I ask you something?"

"Yeah," he said, smiling at me like I was about to propose or something.

"Has it ever crossed your mind why I never ask any questions when it comes to you?"

"Nope! And could we leave this subject right here?"

When he said that, I quickly said, "Not a problem."

The phone rang. "Hello?"

"Hey, Blu, what you up to girl?" Thad sitting there looking at the TV, but his attention is completely on me.

"I'm not doing too much. Just hanging around the house."

"I called because I wanted to know if you wanted to go out. You don't need any money, because money will be put in your purse, so please don't let that be a reason for you to say No."

"I was going to call you anyway to talk to you about some things."

"Cool! Throw some things in a bag and let me come get you."

"I'll call you back in thirty minutes."

"Why?"

"I need to call Sandy to see if she can bring me to meet you and we'll go from there."

"Whatever you say, Blu, but call me right back."

I dashed out the door and went over to Sandy's. I threw a few pieces I had at her house in a bag, called Starr while in route, for her to meet me at Lenox mall.

"The mall will be closing in a couple of hours, so we have to hurry."

"Starr, you always shopping."

"I know it, and I'm putting you On so you'll always be shopping, too. Blu, what you wearing tonight?"

"I got some jeans and a couple of tops to choose from."

"That's fine, because it's a semi-casual dress code."

"Where we going?"

"I'm feeling brand new today for some reason, so I want some brand new clothes to go with my attitude."

"You be gettin' that money, don't you, Starr?"

"Is it a little bit of trick in that question, Blu?"

"No! My mission is to be right there with you."

"Good, that's all I needed to hear." I'm not sure what Starr meant by that but I will deal with whatever, whenever it comes. Starr turned and looked at me and said, "You are so sexy. You just need to develop the right attitude to go with the way you look. Before we get to the house, let's grab a bite to eat so we can sip on some wine while we get ready."

"Exactly where are we going tonight?"
"Oh, girl, we going only to be among the six-figga fellas, along with the entrepreneur ballers. Let me be the first to say, Blu girl, you looking like a million dollars. Sexy, beautiful, fierce-ass diva is written all over you, with a touch of classy simplicity."

"Wow! Thank you for the compliment, and I must say, Starr, you looking really cute yourself." Just Cute, Blu? Damn, I think I'm the shit, right now! Fuck, cute!

I shook my head and smiled while Starr did her model walk down the hall.

"Okay, Blu, you ready to go?"

"I'm ready, but Starr, can I ask you a question?"

"What?"

"Where are your children?"

"Where are yours?"

"Oh, the twins living with their grandparents for a while."

"Well, so are mine. See, that's what I'm talking about. Your mindset needs to match with your looks, honey. Blu, please leave all of that alone."

"Fine! Just put your seatbelt on, Starsha, since you doing 90 in a 55 mile per hour zone."

Chapter Twelve

"**Excuse me, Waiter**. Please bring the young lady another glass of wine."

"And how do you know I want another glass?"

"I saw you and your friend walk in the door about fifteen minutes ago and you downed the first glass immediately." This guy just don't know how nervous I am. And why the hell is he sweating me? As we pulled into this gated community I thought we were going to a house party—or should I say, mansion party—because these houses are as large as apartment buildings, but we drove to the end of the street and pulled through another set of gates into a beautiful country club swarming with limousines, Range Rovers and Rolls Royces. A team of valet parking attendants met us at our door. Butterflies and bees were fighting for territory in my stomach. When we left the condo, Starr had already put $600 in my purse to go with the $14 I already had. On the way to the party she told me that when we made our way in I should just mingle and we'd find each other when it was time for her to introduce me to some people. I was nervous as hell, so I grabbed a drink ASAP.

"Well, the reason I downed that glass of wine immediately was that I've just had a very long day."

"My name is Royce Jackson, but you can call me R.J. And yours?"

"I'm Blu Spencer, but you can call me Blu."

"I'm sure you've been told that Blu is a very unusual name, but pretty none the less."

"People often ask questions about my name, and I tell them it's just a name my momma gave me."

"Excuse me. I'm Starr—better known as Blu's best friend. And you are?" My name is RJ!

 And how are you this evening Ms. Starr?"

"Never better! But I have to steal my girl away for a few."

"No problem. Hopefully we can continue our conversation later, Blu."

I gave him a look that said, "We'll see."

"Victor, I'd like you to meet Blu." I hope Starr not trying to set me up with anybody. Victor immediately asked if we would join him in a photograph. There were cameramen everywhere.

Star whispers to me, "Smile, girl, for every photo. Own the shot." We were in picture after picture. NFL and NBA players were here that I recognized along with a few celebrities. The glass of wine in my hand, plus the three that went before it, have me completely relaxed and feeling just as important as the rich and famous around me. [Starr had already informed me that she was the agent for a couple of NBA players and their wives, and one contact had lead to another, so here we are—or rather here she is again.

"Are you game for the afterparty?"

"Oh, so you telling me there's a party after this party?"

"You spending the night at my house, Blu, so relax and let's just enjoy ourselves."

"Okay, I'm game."

"Everybody here knows Victor in some shape, form or fashion. He's a movie director, among other things. I haven't run across a woman who wouldn't mind exploring on any level with him."

"What about you, Starr?"

"I could have him, but it would only be for a night. He's not offering much more than that to anybody. Besides, the respect between us is simply because I won't take advantage of that offer."

After taking tons of pictures, meeting lots of people, eating good food and drinking plenty, we were heading to the hotel, but Starr said we need to run to the condo first. "Blu, let's change our clothes and make an appearance. They've seen us in these outfits all evening and we've taken dozens of pictures. A lot of these people plus some newcomers will be there, so let's change." I freshened up a bit and put on a Dolce and Gabbana strapless dress that Starr pulled

out of her closet and still had the $800 tag
on it. I put my strappy black and diamond
stilettos back on that I'd worn with the
hip-hugger jeans earlier. Starr had on a
sexy little cocktail dress with spaghetti
straps.

As we walked from the elevator Starr said,
"Well Kiss My Ass! He has bought the whole
floor for tonight."

"Simply Beautiful!" was all Victor said when
we walked into the hotel suite. "Let me
introduce you to my brother. Royce, this is
Starr, and this is Blu."

"Nice to meet you!" Starr quickly said.

"So we meet again, Ms. Blu!"

"Oh, y'all know each other?" Victor asked,
surprised.

"No, not really, I just met R.J. at the party earlier tonight."

Victor and R.J. favor a lot, except, Victor is short as hell and RJ is about six one. Both are brown skin and have low haircuts. They both look ordinary, nothing fancy, smell so good and wear the latest designer gear for men.

"Ms. Lady, can we talk?" R.J. asked me while my back was turned getting me a drink. I just stood there and sip my wine, never turning around to face him. "Blu, let me leave you my card so you can call me. I would ask you for your number but the vibe I'm getting from you says that won't happen." R.J. is so close behind me all in my ear and I am loving it.

"R.J., where are you going with this conversation?"

"Yes, I'm attracted to you, but so is every other guy in here, they were all digging you at the country club. You never look twice at one guy, not even me. You beautiful, you fine, and mysterious as hell. Blu, you not looking for anything, are you?"

"No, I'm not, as a matter of fact I'm not looking for any*one*, either." I walked away as if R.J. wasn't standing behind me. Starr was working the room. I hated to tell her how I was ready to go, but she beat me to the punch as soon as she saw me.

"You ready to call it a night, Blu?"

I quickly replied, "Yes, ma'am."

Chapter Thirteen

I decided to catch the train all the way home. I wanted to think about the night before and sightsee like a tourist. After falling straight to sleep last night at Starr's place, I feel alright. I'm walking in slow motion to the door but still got here fast.

"You finally remember where you live?"

"Are you asking or telling me? Due to the fact that you've taken everything but the breath in my body, I really am not concerned with anything dealing with you."

"What is that supposed to be? Some kind of reverse psychology?

Take your clothes off, Blu."

"For what, Thadius? Let's not do this. Please stop, Thad!"

"If I start putting some heat in your ass, will you cooperate then?" He pulled out what looked like a 9mm gun. He pressed the barrel against my inner thigh and said, "Now, take your clothes off." I slowly took everything off and he forcefully started fucking me.

After jerking off he snatched himself out and hit me across the face with the gun. At first I held my face, then I started to get up and he kicked me in my back and I fell to the floor. "Where you think you going?" I was so relieved to see him dress quickly, grab a beer from the fridge and just leave. To the best of my ability I got up, took a shower, dressed, packed a bag and called Sandy. "Hey, Sandy, it's Blu. I was calling to touch bases with you. Call me when you get this message." I called a cab to take me to the Courtyard Hotel and used four hundred of the six hundred dollars Starr had given me to get myself a room for the week. I felt a whole mixture of emotions. I'm tired. I mean, I am too tired of this "life" with Thad.

I ordered room service and relaxed with the radio on a slow jam station. The phone woke me up with Sandy on the other end all hysterical and shit.

"Hey Blu, what's wrong? Where are you? Are you okay?"

"Slow down, Sandy. I'm okay. What are you doing, other than having a panic attack?"

"Oh, I was sleeping when you called. I took some pills to help with my period. You know this time of the month have me messed up."

"Well, I'm at the Courtyard for a week or so until I figure out my next move."

"Girl, you left Thad?"

"It seems that way, don't it? But I'll see what happens."

"Good! Whatever you need, Blu. You know I'm here."

"I know, and I'll see you sometime this week. Thank you, Sandy, for always being here for me."

"Don't mention it. Talk to you later."

"Bye."

It's been three days already in this hotel. I talk to the manager yesterday and gave him a little story on why I need to live here for a while and ask him if I could work to earn my stay. He agreed not only to let me stay for free, but give me a nice cash paycheck to take room service calls from my room for a few hours a week.

The manager of the hotel is a white guy that looks like he got a little black in him. His name is Cornelius Hudson, but he's known as Mr. C. He has black hair and eyes with a black goatee and a pretty white smile. He looks to be in his mid-thirties. I know he is very interested in me. *Ring. Ring.* Now who's calling? Nobody knows this number.

"Hello?"

"I hope I didn't catch you at a bad time, Ms. Spencer. This is Mr. C."

"Oh, Hi. No, it's okay. What can I do for you?"

"Would you like to meet me in the dining room for dinner?"

"But it's closed."

"I know, that's why it's perfect. What do you like to eat, Blu? Excuse me, can I call you Blu?"

"Sure you can, and whatever you choose is fine. I'm pretty open. I'll be down in about twenty minutes."

WOW! Mr.C got candles lit, music playing and a waitress just brought out wine and asked me to choose from the menu. He's just sitting across the table with a smile on his face. "Order anything you like, sweetheart." I kept it simple and ordered a Caesar salad, steak and lobster. He ordered the same. I'm lonely as hell, and he looks just as lonely, so after we laughed talked and looked in each other's eyes, I graciously removed myself from the temptation, thanked him for dinner and said I should be going to my room. He understood and said goodnight.

Chapter Fourteen

The vibration of my phone woke me up.

Damn. Where is it?

"Hello."

"Hey, Blu."

"Oh, hey, Starr."

"Were you asleep?"

"Yeah, but I'm up now. I was planning to call you this morning anyway."

"I called to see if you want to do lunch or something. You know, our usual. And I'll get you from the train station, I know that's the only way you do it."

"Actually, I'm at the Courtyard downtown, so you can come here."

"Oh, okay. What's that about?"

"Tell you all about it when you get here."

"So Blu, what's this all about?"

"Can you just drive, and when we get where we're going I will tell you."

"You wanna order in or go out? Now, Blu, You know me, I prefer to order in."

"Okay, that's cool. Let me get a glass of wine."

"You read my mind. While we wait on our food, lets talk."

"Okay, Starr, long story short: I left my girls' dad, and hopefully I won't have to look that way again."

"Get the fuck out of here! Are you serious?"

"Yep."

"Is that how you got that bruise on your face?"

"It's going away, so never mind that. So, how are you and your friend?"

"Pretty much the same. Well, Blu, he did come over the other day with a gash on his hand. He told me he had to slap somebody about his business. I said, 'Damn, all that came from a slap?' He said, yeah, he hit him with his gun.

Normally I wouldn't give a shit, but he was acting like such a baby and wanted me to doctor on it. Anyway, Blu, on another note, when the last time your man made love to you or fucked you good?

"The 'made love' part I'm not even addressing, I don't even know what that is. And me getting 'fucked good' hasn't happened either."

"Okay, Blu, hear me out. I want you to have some pleasure. You know, relax, feel good and come away from all your worries for a while. I'm your BFF, remember? I see the unhappiness and stress all in your face."

"Starr, can we please drop this conversation? You need to let me worry about what dick I'm getting' or not getting'."

"Relax, Blu. We just having girl talk." Starr's phone rang and she picked it up on the very last ring. She went to the back to take the call. Starr yelled from her bedroom, "Blu, I need to meet my friend, and it won't take long, so why don't you hang around here until I get back?"

"Naw, I think I'ma head back to the hotel and let's just hook up again in a couple of days."

"Are you sure? I would love for you to ride with me, but he so funny about running into anybody because of our obligations."

"Oh, I understand completely. We'll talk later."

The message light is blinking on the phone in my room. It can only be one person.

"Hi, Mr. C. What's up?"

"Hello, Blu. I wanted to know if you'd have dinner with me tonight? Are you free?"

"Sure, why not!"

"Instead of eating in the dining room, I'd really like to take you out."

"Okay, let's make it around 8:00. Is that good for you?"

"Yeah, that's perfect."

I hung up the phone, turned on some slow jams, and lit a few candles before slipping into the tub with the jets going. Wow, what a drastic change from my life not long ago.

My mind is overwhelmed with all sorts of thoughts.

"Would you like a booth or a table?"

"A booth, please," I said quickly before Mr. C. could say anything.

"Please, call me Cornelius. Mr. C. is what I'm called at work, and I don't want to feel like we're working."

"Cornelius, are you trying to date me or what?"

"You are a beautiful woman, Blu. First, let me say that as far as your room goes, you don't have to work in room service because I took care of your bill for the entire month."

"Why? Why did you do that? And at what price for me?"

"Let's just say that I help people when and where I can. Blu, I can tell you really need somewhere to go. I don't know what's going on in your life, but you aren't staying at a hotel just because it's something you like to do. Besides, I want to help. No strings attached, I swear. It's a coincidence that I'm attracted to someone I happen to be helping."

"I think you're nice, too. It's just I have to find my way right now, and I don't have time for romantic hassles or dealing with a relationship."

"I understand. From here on out, it's strictly platonic. I truly want to be of any kind of help to you that I can."

"Thank you, Cornelius. Let's enjoy our dinner."

I'm definitely not complaining, but I find it ironic that I haven't heard from Thadius at all. Starr left me a voicemail saying she would be out of town for a few days and would call me as soon as she returns. It's seven a.m. Who the hell is knocking at my door? It's too early for housekeeping.

"Who is it?"

"It's R.J."

"Who?"

"R.J." I'd heard him the first time. I wonder why he's here? It's no mystery how he knows where I am. I totally forgot that it was New Year's Day. When I spoke with my children I didn't make mention of it, and they didn't either.

"Come on in, R.J. What brings you here?" He sat at the little table with an unusual smile on his face. For a moment I stood and looked at him and shook my head, trying to figure out what he want with me. I had on some panties and a wife beater and didn't bother to put on anything prior to letting him in.

Out of nowhere R.J. says, "Blu, are you seeing anybody?"

"No, are you?"

He threw a line at me, saying, "Now I am." I caught it, not caring about the meaning behind it. While I was looking at him, the thought came to me that I have reached the turning point in my life where I'm on my own terms, making my own rules, with No apology's.

"You showed up with the sunrise, so you want some breakfast?" We ordered room service, sat and talked. We ordered lunch, sat and talked. We spent the rest of the day watching movies and sipping on some Henn and coke. I was completely mellowed out and really ready for him to leave. I start saying things like, "I guess I'll get ready for bed," and "I'm glad you spent the day with me." I even start yawning. R.J. completely ignored me and turned toward me, grabbed my hand and pulled me close to him, saying, "You don't want me to go, but even more so, I don't want to go."

I didn't say anything. We kissed and embraced like we were long overdue. I pulled back. "Okay, I'll talk to you another time."

"Aight," he said. "I get the picture."

"Goodnight!" Closing the door behind him. *That was close*!

What the hell is really going on? It's not even eight o'clock a.m. and I hear knocking at door. I look through the peephole, it's

R.J. again, standing there looking anxious and weird at the same time. "Who is it?"

"It's me, baby."

"Who the hell is me?"

"R.J., that's who."

"What brings you over here, unannounced, again?"

"I'm leaving for L.A. this evening, I wanted to see you before I go. I'll be gone for a week, and I want you to fly out there. If you don't already know, I'm a director and producer of high-end videos for celebrities. I'm over everything, dealing with tours, concerts, etc. My brother Vic is a movie director, so we both behind the scenes in the entertainment world. But back to you. Have you ever thought about a career in entertainment?"

"No, I haven't."

"Blu, you have a body and face to die for, and with the right contacts you could go straight to the top, making your own money on your own terms. I think you are a natural, so I'ma hook you up with one of our assistants who will be your right hand in L.A. and from here on out. I need our focus to stay on us while we together."

"Oh really," I said, not knowing what to make of R.J.'s offer. "You over here at the break of dawn, so let me hop in the shower and slip on some clothes. While in the shower I have my eyes closed just absorbing what R.J. had said. I felt a warm hand go down the middle of my back. He stepped into the shower and kissed me all on my ass, licking between my legs softly, sucking on my skin, whispering over and over, "Where have you been?" We got out the shower, drenched with water, not bothering to dry off. He was so careful with me, as though I might break, caressing me ever so slowly, taking his time and not rushing. His manhood found its way inside of me on its own. We climaxed together after what seemed like hours of loving each other.

We talked and gave a brief overview about our past and what's going on now. R.J. had a six p.m. flight. "Do you know that it's going on three p.m.? Unless you leave now and go straight to the airport you will miss your flight."

"Why don't I change my flight time for tomorrow evening, and you roll out with me instead of catching a flight in a couple of days?"

"I can do that."

"Cool. Let's take a shower and go get something to eat. We'll get you some things to travel with, baby girl."

This day had come before I knew it. I felt so important packing all my new things in my new Louis Vuitton luggage. The Limo picked us up on time, I feel like a star. Now that we have boarded the plane as first class passengers of course, I'm in awe about it all. I'm owning it though, like I've never known any other way.

Chapter Fifteen

This can't be anybody but Starr calling.

She's the only one that has my new number.

"Hey, Starr, what's up?"

"No, the question is what's up with you, Ms.
L.A.!"

"I know, right? I can't believe it either. I
guess a thanks is in order, even though you
did send R.J. to my hotel room. He could
have been on some other shit, but good thing
he wasn't. So, thank you, Starr."

"So, Blu, you mind doing a little shopping
for me? I need you to pick up some things
for my friend's kids."

"No problem. I can do that. Just email
me the information and I'll FedEx everything
to you."

"Oh, Wow! Email you! Okay then." Starr sounded proud and impressed at the same time.

I'm staying in a suite at the Ritz Carlton in Downtown L.A. I put on a pair of fitted APO jeans, sheer top and my red bottoms with the four-inch heel. I grab my bag and called for the limo. I went to my meeting at Cover Girl and then to the interview for a spread in Essence Magazine. R.J. has lined up a couple other gigs. I don't even feel like my old self anymore. I'm definitely not like little Blu back in Atlanta. My meeting felt like a success, and my whole life looks like it's falling into place. Let me call R.J. and see what his evening looks like. Damn! Voicemail. "Hey, R.J., it's Blu. Call me when you get a free moment. Talk to you soon. Bye." I guess I'll grab some wine and mail off these things for Starr, then head to the hotel because I really don't know anybody, and I just want to relax and take all of this in.

I ran a hot bath after lighting candles all around the tub. These jets are making a million bubbles, so I turned them off while sipping on my wine. Shit! I left my cell phone on the bed. I jumped out the tub, I know it's R.J. calling me back. "Hello."

"Well, well, well. Look at you. You just done fucked your way all the way to the top."

"Hello?" I said again, as if I didn't know the voice on the other end. Thadius must've gotten the number from his mother. "Oh, hi Thad."

"Is that all I get?"

"What the hell do you want? You've gotten enough from me."

"Listen at you, all high class and shit."

"I'm just doing me, trying to build a solid foundation for me and my girls."

"I don't know what you building, but the girls stay where they are, and that's non-negotiable."

"Whatever!" I hung up before he had a chance to reply. Thad call back, but I let the voicemail get it, I turned off the phone so I wouldn't let him steal my joy.

I'm almost sure the phone ringing in my room is R.J. I didn't even say hello before R.J. is saying "What's up, baby? How'd your day go?"

"It went very well, and I'm so excited. It looks like I will be in Los Angeles for a minute, huh?"

"Yeah, at least for the next two months. But you can commute and do turnaround trips when you want to. With what you're doing, Blu, you will pretty much know your schedule up front."

"Well, R.J., I do need to fly back to handle unfinished business at the hotel."

"I understand all that. But on another note, I'ma come through there in a few, all right?"

"Okay! I'm not going to start shooting for the magazine until next week, so I will book my flight out for the day after tomorrow.

As soon as I opened the door, R.J. wrapped his arms around me, reminding me of everything he love about me. Immediately we went at it non-stop for at least an hour with no break, not even to switch positions. Hell, we never did change positions, just looked in each other's eyes with him telling me his feelings from start to finish.

"Did you order room service?"

"No, did you?"

"Blu, how could I order?"

"I don't know, you could have ordered on your way up here. R.J., just answer the door, because I don't know who it could be."

A bad feeling came over me when I laid eyes on Starr. "Hey, what's up?" R.J. said in an upbeat kind of way.

"Hi, R.J. I'm sorry for popping in on you guys, but, Blu, I really need to talk to you." We standing there looking at Starr with only robes on, and I'm sure sex is written all over us.

"Aight, ladies. I'ma get dressed and head on out so you can talk."

"No, you stay, and Blu, you can come downstairs to the room I got here."

"Baby, I'm ordering me some food and kick back. I will see you when you come back."

I took a quick—or should I say—'whore' shower and put on a true religion jean jumper and my havaianas.

"This hotel room is made totally different from mine."

"Never mind that, Blu. I had to leave Atlanta for a day or so until the smoke clear with my friend. Some men came looking for him at my place yesterday and told me I need to lay low until they deal with him."

"Starr, do you know these guys?"

"I kinda know them."

"What is this about, with you and your friend?"

"All I can tell you is it's dealing with money and drugs. I can't really go into much more than that."

I'm sorry you dealing with all of this.
Since you have issues, I won't ask you to
fly back to Atlanta with me. I booked a
flight so I can go square away my business
at the hotel with the manager. He really
looked out for me. Oh, well no, I can fly
back with you Blu. I'm sure I will be fine.
Ok Starr, get yourself together and meet me
in the lobby in the morning and we off to
Atlanta.

Chapter Sixteen

"Hi Mr. C"

"I told you, it's Cornelius. How are you, Blu? And where have you been?"

"I went to get a job, and I got one—out in L.A. Cornelius, I wanted to come back here to close out any debts. You really helped me out, and I am so thankful. I do need to get a room for a couple of days for me and my girlfriend then I'm heading back out to L.A. I will be happy to pay for my room this time."

"As long as I'm the manager, your money is not needed here."

"Okay, okay. Well, Cornelius, I guess we will talk later." Mm-mm-mm. There is just something about that white black man!

"Blu, let's get changed and get a bite to eat and some wine," Starr said in a tired voice.

"That sounds good. I do need to unwind before I go see my children."

"So, tell me, who is this manager to you?"

"Why you ask me that?" I smack my lips with a smirk on my face, leading Starr to believe that Cornelius is something more than just the manager.

"The both of you have that look, like maybe something went on. Or that you want something to go on," she said, smiling.

"He's just a nice guy, and we have become friends. That's all. So, tell me, Starr, what's going on with you?"

"Like I said, I have to lay low for a couple of days. I can't really go into any details with you, but I'm sure it will work out because it always does."

"I hope so. Well, I'm going to see my girls, and we will hook up here at the hotel later, okay?"

"Sounds good, Blu. I'm going to go run an errand or two."

"All right, see you later, girl."

I called Mrs. Glover to let her know I'm coming over in about an hour. I wanted the girls to be ready so we can go hang out for a while. We need some "mommy and me" time!

As I slowly pulled up to the girls' grandmother's house, I'm not sure what my mind is telling me or what my eyes are showing me. I put the gear in park, still looking at my girls running around the front yard. Mrs. Glover was playing with her plants, so it seem. I yelled from the car,

"My goodness! Look at Zoey and Sky! Aren't you two the most beautiful girls in the world." They were so excited to see me. Mrs. Glover even gave me a hug that told me she'd missed me. I talk with Mrs. Glover for a minute, but I still couldn't take my eyes off the girls. Of course I miss them, but the clothes they had on just blew me away. Their outfits were not even available in the South yet. As a matter of fact, they were the exact outfits I sent to Starr for her man's kids when I was in L.A. The girls are pulling and tugging at me. They are asking me a thousand questions, but I hardly hear them because these are the outfits I know were sent from Los Angeles by me—to Starr.

I'm so confused, and my mind is racing, asking myself if it could possibly be a coincidence. Okay, time to snap out of it. The girls and I are going to the spa, then wherever they wanna go. "All right, girls! Let's ride and go have some fun!" I keep telling myself to get it together because I am just outdone by what my babies have on.

After the spa, we decided to go see my grandmother and take her to dinner with us. Lord knows I wanna be with my children. However, I need some answers to these questions racing through my head. The day was winding down and I had a talk with the girls about everything I'm doing and plan to do. It's all good. I took them back to their Granma's house and headed back to the hotel. I'm anxious to meet back up with Starr. On the other hand, I'm not ready to deal with what I'm thinking. I stopped at a sports bar and had a drink while collecting my thoughts. I hear a loud familiar laugh coming from a table around the corner. Damn, is that Sandy? I followed the sound of her voice.

"Girl, I knew that was you!" We hugged and kissed cheek to cheek. I wasn't sure who the guy was, with Sandy. I'll wait and let her tell me later.

"Mason, I would like you to meet Blu."

"Hello, Blu." You are even more beautiful than Sandy raved about."

"Awww, thank you," was all I could say, seeing that I was curious as hell as to who he was and what Sandy was doing with him.

"Well, I will let you two get back to your evening."

Sandy whispers in my ear, "Oh, no, girl. It's not like that. We will chat later Ms. Blu."

"Okay, Sandy. Just call me." I went back to the bar and ordered another drink. After

157

being at the bar for what seemed like hours, I headed back to the hotel to get some sleep.

I probably should've gotten two rooms instead of this double bed room. I drop my purse and keys on one side of the bed and then flop down on the other side. I can hear soft music and smell the scented candles coming from the bathroom.

"Blu, is that you?"

"Yeah, who else?"

"Come in here for a minute. How was your visit with the twins?"

"My girls are great, more beautiful than ever. I'm tired as hell, though, and I got a lot on my mind."

"A penny for your thoughts, Ms. Blu."

"I was going to wait until morning to talk to you because I'm so tired, but now is as good a time as any."

"Before you start, why don't you pour yourself a glass of wine and hop on in with me."

"Hop on in? Are you bathing or just having a Jacuzzi moment?" I already knew the answer to the question. I was coming out of my clothes, pouring myself that glass of wine. I stood there naked and gulped down the first glass, then poured a second to just sip and talk. Starr looked mesmerized, starring at my body. At that moment I couldn't help but look into Starr's eyes and think back on our friendship from the time we met.

"What's wrong, Blu? Wait! Don't answer that question yet."

"No! I do need to answer that question right now. First of all, Starr, what is your guy friend's name?"

"Why? Why do you need to know that?"

"Just answer the fucking question, Starsha."

"He's known by the name Glover."

"What kind of car does he drive?" I'm standing here naked as hell but seriously asking Starr these questions.

"I will answer that in a minute, but not before I tell you that I'm in love with you, Blu."

"What does you being in love with me have to do with the issue at hand? And anyway, what are you in love with?"

"I love everything about you, Blu. I always have, from day one."

"Well, I'm already committed."

"To who?"

"Men, Bitch! Now, I'm going to ask you again. What kind of car does your man drive?" I know what Starr wants. I'm standing here looking at this chic face-to-face, and thinking to myself, *What the hell? If she wanna eat my cookie, why not?*

What the hell am I thinking? I don't even like women at all, but fuck it. I need to release and relax for a minute, then I will deal with this soon-to-be issue that I have. I stepped into the Jacuzzi after finishing another glass of wine. I sat on the edge of the tub, listening to Starr tell me in a whisper to relax about a hundred times. I had one leg on the step going into the tub and the other propped up on the edge of the Jacuzzi. Starr licked that space right between the main hole and the ass hole.

Okay, That Done It! I can't do this! I got out of the tub and wrapped up in a towel. I sat on the little stool, took a deep breath and said, "Starr, what kind of car does your man drive? You know what? Don't even answer that, because I'm tired. Does the bastard drive a Range Rover? Does he have two daughters? Is his name Thadius? Last name Glover?"

"Hold on, Blu. Slow down." Starr looked at me seeming to be just as surprised as I was. She got out of the tub and put on her robe. She sat on her bed and I sat on mine.

"The clothes I sent you from L.A., my girls had them on today. Now that I think back, I can recall a few instances that put all of this into perspective. You knew he had someone and kids with somebody. Is that why you are in hiding with the relationship?

Damn, Starr! I've always been very private about him because I didn't and don't want to know him anymore. So I wasn't trying to let anyone else know him—at least not through me or in my world in any way. Believe it or not, I'm actually not mad at you because you didn't know it was me, just like I didn't know it was you. I just need a day to take it all in, okay? You keep this room and I'm getting another one. I'll come back tomorrow and get my stuff. Don't worry Starr, I know you didn't know it was me." I gave her a hug to tell her it would be okay, but before I could turn her loose she grabbed me tight and said, "I'm sorry Blu, but I've always known."

Chapter Seventeen

I wonder if Starr can read the expression on my face, because I'm speechless. I pushed her away from me, looked her up and down, grabbed my purse and keys, and walked out. I went to the lobby and asked for another room. "Actually," I said, "I'll take one of those suites. And some wine to be brought up ASAP." When I got on the elevator, the only thing I could think of at that moment was, *What a sight for sore eyes!*

"Hello, Ms. Spencer. Where are you headed? Your room is on the other side."

"Yes, it was, but I'm in the suite for the next two days until I return to Los Angeles."

"You want some company?"

"Yes, I would love some company." I put the key card in the door, and when I opened it, "Wow!" was all I could say.

Cornelius said, "Yes, these suites are really nice."

I don't even want to look at the Jacuzzi. I told Cornelius to relax and wait on the wine to arrive. "I'm going to take a quick shower."

"Blu, would you like to order some food?"

"Yes, that's cool. Whatever you get is fine." My cell phone is ringing off the hook.

"Would you like me to get that?"

"Yeah, right! I don't think so. Just let it ring, Mr. C. These are really nice robes." Cornelius handed me some wine after pouring it into a nice tall wine glass. He poured himself some. We took a sip, looking at each other as if we'd really missed one another.

"So, tell me, Blu. Who or what are you running from this time?"

"Nothing, and no one, thank you very much. I needed some privacy and a little down time away from my friend, Starr, that's all. Excuse me, I have to answer this call. Hello?"

"Hey, angel face, what's up with you?

"Oh, hi."

"Is that all you got for me?"

"Hello, R.J., How you doing?"

"I'm good. I been calling you like crazy, though. Are you on schedule to be back in L.A. day after tomorrow?"

"Yes, I am."

"Okay, baby. I will pick you up from the airport."

"That's fine. Talk to you later. Okay, bye R.J. Now, where were we, Mr. C.?"

"You were just about to tell me what you're running from."

"No, I wasn't, and besides, I'm not running from anything. I thought I told you that." I changed the subject because Cornelius was trying to go to a place where I wasn't willing to go. "These stuffed mushrooms are so good. The salad is great, too, and the wine. In case I forget to say thank you, I'm putting it out there now."

"Blu, you are more than welcome." What he said was followed by a kiss on my lips. He kissed my neck so softly, whispering in my ear, "You are so beautiful, and I care about you so much. I think I may even be in love with you."

"Mr. C., don't say that. I can't handle this, at least not tonight anyway." What the fuck is going on? What's with all this love shit? "Come on, Cornelius. Let's just enjoy the moment."

"That's exactly what I'm doing, Blu, by sharing what's on my mind. Or, should I say, what's in my heart."

"You are a wonderful man, and a true friend, but I got a lot going on right now, and I honestly can't do this."

"Well, can you do this?" He rubbed my hair so gently, I only had a robe on, I just let it drop to the floor. Cornelius laid me gently on my stomach and started kissing me on my feet. He licked all the way up the back of my legs. He bit my butt, not too hard, and licked and kissed my back. My eyes stayed closed, taking it all in, as he instructed me to do. Although I'm not in love with him, I feel like we made love. He held me and we said nothing. I think Cornelius knew I needed the silence, and he respected that. Before I knew it, morning had arrived. We laid there until around ten o'clock.

"Shouldn't you be getting off to work?"

"Yes, but I want to stay here until, well, just until." I knew exactly where he was coming from. I smiled. It was twelve noon. "Ms. Blu, are you hungry? You must be."

"After my bath I'll grab something, and I will call you a little later."

"When are you leaving for L.A.?"

"I told you, tomorrow. I'll be back and forth until I can get situated either here or there." As Mr. C. was leaving he made a comment, saying, "When all is said and done, I'll still be here waiting for you.

Nonchalantly I said, "Uh huh. Yeah."

I almost hate to go to Starr's room. I need to get all my things, but that comes along with facing what I left the night before. When I stepped in the room, seeing her slumped in the Lazy Boy chair holding a glass of wine I didn't feel any remorse at all. The room is a mess, she looks like she's been up all night. Clothes are everywhere. I couldn't help but think to myself that this shit is almost comical. I grudgingly smiled but that faded quickly. "Starr, the last thing you told me was that you've known for a long time that we were with the same man."

"Well, I figured it out a long time ago, but by that time, I was already strongly feeling you, Blu."

"Honestly, Starr, I don't know which way to turn with this whole thing. On one hand, I want detail from detail and answers to my million questions. On the other hand, I really want to just throw my hands up, turn my back, and continue to move forward doing what I do.

"Blu, my feelings for you have not changed. I meant every word."

"I could care less about your feelings and what your words meant. I'm really aggravated by the fact that you are mild mannered as hell toward this shit. I don't trust you anymore, Starr."

"Blu, you need to stop with the soap opera mentality. Grow up and get over it." This bitch is going on and on. I'm so pissed off right now. Starr's voice is fading in the air. I can only hear my own thoughts: *No, this bitch ain't trying to tell me anything about what to do, let alone what to feel.* "Blu, have I not been a true friend to you? I have been there, always concerned and my door has always been open to you on every level. Yes, I've fallen for you in the process, but that still hasn't changed the fact that we are still best friends. I've wanted to tell you all of this for so long, but I just couldn't risk losing your friendship."

"Don't you understand, Starr, that when I found out, instead of you being honest and telling me, that everything changed?" I grabbed all of my stuff and went back to my suite. For the first time in a long time, I called Thadius, my girls' daddy. There wasn't any answer. I wanted to leave a message for his dog ass, but what would I say? So I just hung up. The phone rang back. "Hello?"

"What's up, baby?"

"Oh, I'm getting everything in order so I can be heading that way tomorrow." R.J. sounded so sexy on the phone.

"My brother wants you to audition to possibly co-star in a movie. I'm not talking about the big screen, but it will be aired on Lifetime. What do you think?"

"Wow! That sounds great. I will call you when I get to town and get settled in."

"I got a better idea. Why don't I pick you up from the airport? I miss you, Blu, and I need to see you."

"That's fine."

"I will be at the doors in front of baggage claim in the morning."

"I will see you then, R.J."

"I can't wait, angel face." I took a little nap. The phone rang and woke me up. I said hello without even opening my eyes.

"You calling me, so I guess that mean you must need me for something." I ignored Thadius's snarl. A simple hello would have worked, but I know not to expect that from him.

"I found out about you and Starsha. Starr, whatever you may call her. I'm not surprised, but I *am* pissed about it.

In Thad's typical, careless way he says, "Why are you coming at me with this?" I knew then to leave it alone and tell him goodbye because I am above and beyond anything dealing with Thad. Now he keeps calling, leaving back-to-back messages. I am so not interested in whatever he has to say. I turned my phone off and left it in the suite. I haven't eaten all day with all this drama surrounding me. After I threw something on I went to the hotel bar and ordered some food and a glass of wine. I didn't feel like being alone in my room.

"Hey babe."

"Hi Cornelius. Do you live at this hotel?"

"No, ma'am, I don't."

"Well, you are here all the time from what I can see."

"I have a home, Ms. Blu, but I live alone, so I'm here a lot for various reasons."

"Oh, okay."

"Why don't you grab your food and drink to go?"

"To go where?"

"We can go to my house, since you've never been there," he said, smiling, "or we can just go to your suite. You're leaving tomorrow, right?"

"Right, I will meet you in my suite in one hour."

Chapter Eighteen

"**You smell so** good, Blu. Where are your clothes?"

"I would love to be asking you the same question, Mr. C., but that won't happen, being that you still have them on."

"Well, let me fix that." I sat and watched while Cornelius slowly undressed. He has to be the finest white man I've ever seen, let alone talked to. "Damn!" is all I can say. I've never felt something this good and so right at the same time. Every time this man touch me I feel some kind of love from him. My eyes stayed closed the entire time Cornelius and I were making love, having sex, or whatever the title was for this.

"Wake up, Mr. C.! I have to get to the airport."

"Please stay one more day, Blu."

"I can't. I have to go, because I have appointments. I will be back in a couple of weeks, I promise."

"Will you at least call me while you're out there?"

"Yes, definitely." I took a shower, dressed, and headed to the airport. As I board the plane, I couldn't help but think of Starr. I left without saying goodbye or anything. She is really too much for me. Between her being Thad's Bitch and she trying to make me her Bitch, I'm just outdone by it all. However, on the flip side, me and this girl have some type of friendship, I think.

"Ms. Spencer, would you like something to drink?"

"Yes, please. Could I get some Tylenol, as well?"

"Sure, coming right up." The flight attendant gave me an extra pack of Tylenol for later. I'm sitting back in my chair, struggling with my thoughts. At this very moment, all I can think of is how Thad has hurt me. This man has never been faithful. I often think of two things concerning myself. My past tells me that I'm damaged goods. My present and future tell me that I'm a diamond in the rough. My mind is in deep thought mode about everything surrounding my world right now. I need something or someone to help me clear my mind. All these mixed emotions and thoughts are mentally exhausting me. The "fasten seatbelts" sign popped on, breaking my train of thoughts. The captain came on the intercom, letting us know the plane was descending and we would be arriving at LAX momentarily.

R.J. usually greets me with a smile, hug, and a kiss. I must say, I can't wait to see him, although this feeling for Cornelius is very strong. Like I really need to be torn between two men right now! It seems like a million people are standing at baggage claim. I have such distinctive luggage to where I can spot them anywhere easily. This belt has gone around at least three times and I don't see my luggage nowhere. I hear a voice behind me similar to the voice I heard long time ago at the country club Starr and I attended, when and where all this got started.

"Are you looking for these?"

I felt my heart beat a little faster as I turned around and looked into his sweet brown eyes and warm smile.

"As a matter of fact, I am."

"Hello, R.J. How are you, darling?"

"As always, angel face, I'm as good as it gets. I'm double parked, so we have to get a move on." As we rode down the freeway, R.J. had a thousand questions. "So, tell me, Blu. What are you planning on doing about this expensive hotel you living in like an apartment? If you are ready, baby girl, I found a little spot for you."

"Really, Is that right? I'm going to make a move soon. I just got a lot of shit to sort out in my head."

"Like what?" with his forehead wrinkled up looking puzzled as hell but definitely waiting on an answer.

"Like I said, R.J., I have to sort some things out, then I will be ready, okay?"

"Ummm, okay. Blu, are you bringing your kids to L.A.?"

"R.J., please! Leave it alone already." Soon as I opened the door to my hotel room I dropped my bags and flopped on the bed. I appreciated the silence while R.J. rubbed my back, it made me realize how tired I am. It's dark outside and I'm just waking up. No R.J. in sight, but the note he left says he will call me later.

I have a meeting coming up with Victor Jackson who is a movie director/producer and R.J.'s brother. I can't seem to get it together today. I'm hanging around in my Victoria's Secret teddy and slipper socks. My hair has grown a lot. I get it pressed and wear it straight. That's big for me, because my hair is naturally curly. I'm going to get my first relaxer at my hair appointment tomorrow. Continuing to get my hair pressed is no longer the move. My phone hasn't rung all day.

"Hello, Ms. Blu."

"Hello to you, Mr. C. I haven't talk to you in a while."

"And whose fault is that?"

"I'm so busy, Cornelius, but if I could see you right now, I would. I have thought a lot about you since the other day."

"So if you had the chance right now to see me, would you take it?"

"Of course I would, but I'm getting ready for..."

"Hush, Blu, and open the door."

Chapter Nineteen

"**Oh my god**, Cornelius. What are you doing here?"

"I had to see you, baby. I tried to give you your space and let you call me but I felt like you were never going to call." I was speechless and just let my eyes smile at Cornelius. We embraced each other and it felt so right. "Now doesn't this feel like we belong together?"

"Come on, let's not go there, okay?" I continued hugging him until we were taking off each other's clothes in silence. He backed me up until I fell on the chair and then start sucking my toes, working his way up. Once he reached between my legs, he grazed my clitoris with his warm tongue feeling like a feather was tickling me then slowly grabbing it with his lips. Cornelius sucked and pulled it gently towards him. He passionately tongue kissed my clitoris, allowing it to harden, and just as he applied a little pressure, I came in his mouth as he licked and swallowed, being sure not to leave anything behind.

"It's so good, baby," is what he said, before entering inside of me. I could feel his dick pulsating while he long stroked all the way in and out, over and over. He then turned me over and start sexing me from the back. Once I felt him start to cum I quickly turned over and got on top so he can look in my eyes while he came. I allowed myself to cum again. We lay there still in silence with me having tears roll down my face.

"What's wrong, sweetie?"

"Nothing."

"What do you mean, nothing?"

"I'm okay. Honestly, I am."

"Blu, you always hold everything in. That's not healthy, sweetheart. I know you are a strong woman and you have been through a lot, but baby, you have to let all that stuff out."

"Cornelius, just let it go." He just shook his head, agreeing, and grabbed me tight, rubbing my back. "How long are you here?"

"Well, I was going to determine that by whatever you had to say about my pop-in visit."

"Oh, well, I have a meeting tomorrow."

"I thought you said in two days? So, that's the day after tomorrow. That means you can spend tomorrow with me, and then I'll head back to Atlanta so I can make sure they're running my hotel right."

"What do you mean, your hotel? Aren't you the manager?"

"Yes, I am. I guess it's safe to let you know that I'm also the owner."

"WHAT? Are you serious, Cornelius?"

"Yes, baby, I'm serious. I spend a lot of time there because, like I told you in the beginning, I'm alone and I need something to occupy my mind, so I stay busy at the hotel. Well, at this particular one, anyway, because I actually own ten."

"TEN? Shut The Hell Up! You got to be kidding me. Wow, that's great for you, Mr. C. If things keep going the way that they are for me, my babies and I are going straight to the top. I have learned that there is no way to escape the storms of life, but if you stay strong and don't give up, you will see the light at the end of the tunnel. I know for a fact that after every storm there is a rainbow."

"I couldn't have said it better, Ms. Blu. However, you need to know that I love you, and you have the world at your fingertips, just reach out and grab it. Read between the lines, baby girl, and think about it. It will come to you."

I immediately change the subject. "You wanna get some room service?"

"Whatever you want to do, but wouldn't you like to go out?"

"No, I'm tired, Cornelius. I want to eat, take a bath, climb in bed and watch T.V., sleep or whatever."

He just smiled, "Damn, you do love to eat!"

Cornelius is gone. I'm up early. My meeting is in two hours. My hair has grown as if I never had a haircut. This new relaxer makes it look longer than I've ever seen it. I'm wearing a Ralph Lauren business suit with my Manoloes and handbag to match. I figured I would show my professional side.

Chapter Twenty

"**Good morning, Ms. Spencer**."

"Good morning to you, Mr. Jackson."

"Please, call me Victor. You know we are on a first name basis."

"I was following suit, that's all. And I insist you call me Blu." Victor explained in detail about a screen test. It seemed that he went over a million things. I went for testing that afternoon. I was told that I was a natural along with being absolutely beautiful. I was so proud of everything about today. R.J. hooked me up with one of his assistants when I first came to Los Angeles who is now my personal assistant, a black girl name Charisma who is really good at helping me with everything. She wants to do other things but she's working with me for now. I took my assistant to dinner after such a long day. I went home, or should I say, to my hotel room, afterwards.

"Good morning, baby."

"Good morning, R.J."

"How was your appointment yesterday? You know I want to know all about it, from start to finish."

"Well, it went great. Victor will be in touch with me in a few days."

"I told you, angel face, there is no limit. If you stay focused you will be at the top in no time. You have your Covergirl business under your belt. You've done a photo spread in Essence Magazine, and now you going to be in a movie. Girl! You doing it big. And very fast, I might add."

"Yeah, I'm feeling pretty good about things, thanks to you. I owe it all to you, R.J. You saw something in me and believed it, and then helped me get the confidence and courage I need to do all of this. So I want to say thank you, baby, for all of it. But, I would like to know...why? You haven't asked me for anything or made me feel like there's a catch, so, why, R.J.?"

"Blu, everything doesn't have to be..."

I stopped him before he could finish. "Yeah, okay, we don't have to go there, R.J. It's always something for something in this world we live in."

"In case you didn't know, Blu, I have my own money and lots of it. I'm very well established. I saw a beautiful talent and thought I would help you open some doors that I know you could never open by yourself. No strings attached, other than me being your first and number one fan. He sealed all of that with a kiss and a smile, and I smiled back at him. R.J. wants to have sex right now. I can't, or should I say, I don't want to. Cornelius just left, and my body hasn't come down from that high yet. I...I'm actually missing him already. However I am "feeling" R.J. I appreciate them both. Nonetheless, I feel some type of obligation to R.J., even though he said there are no strings attached. Soon as I sing a different tune that don't include him; that's when I'll see all those invisible strings appear, I'm sure. I tried to change the mood.

"I think I would like to get a condo in Manhattan."

"Why? Blu, don't you like it in L.A.?"

"Yes, it's nice here. I have been looking around in my spare time. I've been on the computer and I hired an agent to research for me."

"Why don't you let your friend, Starr, look around for you? She's a real estate agent."

"Yes, she is, but like I told you, I have an agent looking into some areas for me. Manhattan is where my interest is."

He said, while obviously trying to maintain his composure "Come on Blu, Is that really where you want to raise your girls?"

"If I wasn't sure about what I want to do, R.J., then I would continue to answer these questions. Why don't we get a bite to eat?"

 He said, while trying to smile, "Your lil ass will do anything right about now to escape this conversation." "Whatever! Let's get some food."

"Okay, come on girl. But let me use the restroom first. And you answer that phone, It's ringing off the hook."

"Hello! Hello! Hello!"

"Oh, Wow, did I catch you at a bad time?" After hearing Starsha's voice, I was torn between hanging up or just answering her question. I was silent until she spoke again. "Let me be one of the first to congratulate you on your film."

"Thank you," I said, in a dull voice, after sitting down and crossing my legs. I knew right away that this was going to be a long and unwanted conversation. But I couldn't help but think that if I hadn't met Starsha in the store that day, I wouldn't be where I am with this career and all.

"All I can say at this point, Blu, is that I'm really sorry."

I didn't know whether to get choked up or remind this bitch of what's what and who's who! "Listen, Starr. When it comes to Thadius, he can't be trusted and I know him all too well. But *you*! Well, let me just get back with you."

"Come on, Blu. Yes, I've known. Not the entire time, but yes, I knew prior to you coming to me, and can you stop being so fucking catty please?"

"Are any one of your five, six or seven kids his?"

"No, Blu. He only has the twins."

"Really! Thank you, Starsha, for telling me what the fuck my children's father, my former partner, has or doesn't have."

"Blu, it's like this: I care a great deal about you, however I love Glover. We need to just move on and continue to keep our lives separate in particular when it comes to our men, because that has always worked for us. He and I will not stop seeing each other, simple as that. Now, I'm here for you, Blu, like I've always been when you needed me. So, again, stop being so fucking catty and..."

"Let me interrupt you right there, Starr. You can preach all of what you just said to the choir, Bitch! Okay. With the way I feel about this whole situation, it would be easy to go there with you, but no. From this moment on, I'm going to work on you being a distant memory. If some type of twisted, unexplainable shit were to happen in the future where a phone call would be warranted, then please, let me call you. If for some fucked up reason we run into each other anywhere at any time, then please, act like you don't know me. And be assured that it will be reciprocated." I wanted to slam the phone down on the hook, but you can't do that with a cell phone. I just hung up and turned around to find R.J. leaning against the desk listening, and undoubtedly heard my whole conversation. I had forgotten he was here. Damn! Now he, I'm sure, will want to know the details behind that phone call. As if none of that had just taken place, I said, "Oh, baby, you ready to go?"

He just looked all puzzled and grabbed his keys and extended his hand to the door. While we're on the elevator, R.J. says, "Angel face, let's talk about it when you ready." I nodded my head and we held hands and walked off the elevator.

Chapter Twenty-One

"**Hey Sandy**."

"Blu, is this really you calling me? So you do remember your best friend who's only been your friend since forever."

"Of course I remember you, Sandy, and I miss you like crazy, too. Why don't you come out here to L.A. and hang out for a couple of weeks?"

"Oh, I don't know, Blu."

"C'mon. I will take care of everything. Just pack a bag, honey. How soon can you get to the airport?"

"Girl, I can get there yesterday!" We both laugh, like that was too funny.

"Okay, Sandy, I will call you back tonight with the details. Wait! Before I go, can you be ready by tomorrow?"

"I sure can."

"Okay, I will call you back in a little while, so pack a bag, girl."

I screamed Sandy's name all the way across the airport. My stilettos wouldn't allow me to run like O.J. toward her, so I walked fast as hell until we dropped everything and hug like we were shooting a commercial or something.

I bought Sandy a brand new sewing machine and everything it takes to put it to work. My hotel room looks like an office, fabric store, liquor store, and lingerie store, and somewhere in there we had a corner to sleep in. We talked, laughed, cried and in between all that Sandy was sewing me outfits and of course making clothes and things for her goddaughters. I was learning my lines for my

movie that I'm the lead actress in. For
about a week I didn't take calls or see R.J.
or Cornelius. I felt like I was taking time
to regroup. It was nice. Blu, I sure hate to
leave tomorrow. I could get use to living in
this hotel, eating out all the time and just
plain busy like you. I have to admit, it's
fabulous! I love it all except when I think
about my babies and how we living in
different places. Look at it like this, Blu.
You getting everything in order so they can
be with you for good. Yes, that's true.
Anyway girl, make sure you got everything.
You came with one bag and leaving with four.

It's been a while. Sandy is gone back to
Atlanta. From the first day on set shooting
the movie, everyone is so attentive. My
trailer is stocked with food, decorated with

flowers, and furnished with everything I could ever want or imagine. After we finished the last take and they called for a wrap for the week, I called Mrs. Glover. I needed to talk to her about sending my girls out here for a few days. Of course Sandy will fly with them, being that it's their first time on an airplane. I'm sure she won't have a problem with them coming. I'm always in touch and involved as much as possible, considering. I get them everything they want and need, including satisfying a few of Mrs. Glover's requests as well. However, the fact that they don't have me is heart wrenching sometimes. I can feel the guilt of not being with my girls trying to set in, so let me change my channel of thinking before I get too depressed.

"Hello, Mrs. Glover. How you been doing?"

"Oh, I'm taking one day at a time with these little ladies. Are you doing okay out there in California?"

"Yes...I'm just missing my girls. I can't begin to tell you, Mrs. Glover, how grateful I am that you have taken them and what a great job you've done."

"Well, Blu, you certainly make it easy because the girls and I don't want or need for anything."

"Because of you, I've been able to live out a dream. The girls are getting older and I'm thinking of moving to New York and bringing my children with me."

In a very calm voice, Mrs. Glover says, "Oh, wow. Well, I told you I would take care of my grandkids until you got on your feet. I guess you ready to take back over, huh?"

"Yes, I am, but I was calling to put together a trip for the girls to come out here and visit for a week or so. Are you okay with that?"

"Of course, Blu. I think that would be great for you and for them. I also think they will enjoy the airplane ride probably more than anything."

"Mrs. Glover, I'm going to take them shopping when they get here, plus Sandy made them a few outfits. They would only need to bring a carry-on bag with their personal belongings. Thank god we will skip baggage claim and all that, because that's a drag within itself. And you know my babies will be flying first class."

Mrs. Glover laughs and says, "Oh, honey, I figured that, knowing you, Blu.

And I said, "Yep! Nothing but the best for these little big girls! Do you think getting them ready to come out here in the next couple of days is too soon? Would you need more time?"

Mrs. Glover says, "Well, since they don't have to pack anything really other than personal items, I think we can make that happen."

"Great! I will call you with all the information in the morning. Sandy will meet you guys at the airport because she will be flying back out here with them."

"Okay, Blu. I will talk to you in the morning. And by the way, you just missed Thadius right before you called. I can't even describe the look on my face, but it was a good thing that we were on the phone.

"Oh? And how has he been doing?"

"He's doing good, Blu, and he told me he speaks to you on occasion."

I said, "Well, okay, Mrs. Glover. I will call you tomorrow." I didn't even entertain that lying ass fool, telling his mamma the untruth. "Thank you again for everything."

"You are welcome, Ms. Blu."

I was trying to hurry and get off the phone with her so I could get my other line that had been ringing since I had been on the phone.

"Hello?"

"I been calling you girl, back to back, and you refuse to answer the phone. What are you doing?"

"I was on the phone with my girls, making arrangements for them to come out here, R.J."

"That's real good, baby". "Now I finally get to meet the famous Sky and Zoey."

I just brushed it off with, "Oh yeah, they'll be here in a couple of days." I hadn't thought about how or even if I would introduce my girls to R.J.

"Do you miss me, Blu? Because I miss you so much."

"Yes, I miss you. I been doing some 'me time,' that's all."

"Can I see you today? Like right now?" If he only knew what I was thinking. *Hell yeah you can see me right now! I need to be loved—caressed and all that other shit.*

I asked in a subtle but sexy voice, "Are you on your way?"

He said, "On my way, baby!"

We hung up and I flew like a maniac to my hotel. I knew I had a little time because

R.J. wouldn't be there for at least an hour. I showered and put on a robe because it's no secret what was going to take place when he got there. For some reason anxiety was weighing in on me, so I lit some candles and turned on some music to help mellow me out. Although R.J. always knew what to say, and definitely what to do. That just didn't seem like it would be enough this time.

I was lying back in the recliner and realized this was a good time to call Sandy and discuss the details about my girls while I wait on R.J. to get here.

"Hey, Sandy, what's going on down there?"

"Hi, Blu. I'm doing some sewing along with a little this and a little that."

"I'm calling to discuss you coming back out here with the girls. I'm putting it together for them to travel in the next couple of days. I hope that works for you as well."

"Oh, no! I'm so sorry, Blu, but I can't travel for at least a week and a half. I have two appointments I can't miss, but I think the girls will do fine. I will put them safely on the airplane here and you will be waiting at the other end. Girl, they will be just fine."

"Okay, I think I will do that and I'll call you back." That has to be R.J. at the door and my heart just started racing. "Well, all right, Sandy. Let me call you back." I opened the door and he immediately put his hand over my mouth indicating to me not to say a word. Once again, we let our eyes and body language do all the talking. My robe slid down to the floor. R.J. held his hands on my hips while his lips went from the nape of my neck to my shoulders, barely touching, feeling like a feather gliding, making me want him that much more. He took a long, deep breath, inhaling the scent of my body as if it was some kind of calming mechanism for him. I laid back on the bed with one hand massaging my breast and the other rubbing between my legs. My eyes starred into his as he undressed in front of me. R.J. always love to suck and lick on every inch of my body, putting little red marks on me that look like cherries that have been painted on my thighs and ass. Ironically, his tongue was cold when he licked my clitoris, but the heat from my cat warmed it instantly. He let his dick find its own way and slid right on in, going slow so I can feel every inch. As he strokes me with a lot of force, I thrust my hips into him and we are moaning and holding each other as if one of us might try to get away. He goes fast and hard. I change the pace, and then we do it all over again. He never lets me change positions. R.J. stays on top the entire time, looking into my eyes with a satisfied but somewhat dazed look on his face.

Still, not one word after hours. We both lay there in the juices we created. Wet, even sticky, but we still lay there starring at the candles that were almost burned out. The silence was broken by R.J.'s raspy voice, "I love you. And I want to start talking about taking this thing between us to another level."

It was dead silence in the room. I wanted to say something, but I couldn't. "You don't have to say anything, although I wish you would. Just think about that for a while and I will get back with you on it after your girls leave. I know you getting ready to focus on them right now."

I finally spoke, clearing my throat that was extremely dry. "Yeah, we will talk once they go back to Atlanta. One thing is for sure. I owe it all to you for changing my life, and..."

"Stop! Stop right there, Blu. I need you to only focus on what is between us and that's all. I know you are thankful and all that other stuff when it comes to your career and all, so no need to go there. I only want to focus on us, okay?"

I said "Ok" and left it there. Before I knew it, I could see the sunrise peeking through the drapes. We weren't asleep. R.J. had his head in my lap and neither one of us moved as if we didn't have a care or concern in the world. It felt like time stood still for just a moment for us. I knew I had to be on set and R.J. always has a million and one things to do. I got up and leaned back in the recliner. Watching RJ put his clothes on after showering was like watching a flick. He massaged and lotion his body so seductively. He rubbed and stroked himself smiling at me arrogantly. Damn, RJ! Why can't you just put the lotion and shit on without the show because you're doing way too much. I wanted to tell him to get back in bed but I knew we had to go. After he left, I hurried and put this ass in some water to not just wash it but to cool it off as well.

One of the executive producers must be on her period or something. Her name is Cassie Heatherwood and she getting on my last nerve.

"Take four.

Start from the top, Blu, and this time I
need to see a little more emotion.

 Cut!

 Again! Okay, people, one more time."

 This Bitch is really getting on my damn
nerves. I'm either giving too much emotion
or not enough. I am happy we wrapping up
the first part of this movie. I'm so tired.
I didn't get any sleep last night but I'm
definitely not complaining about that.
Between my breaks today I've been making the
arrangements for my girls to get out here
day after tomorrow. It's a million people
around here. Make-up, hair, wardrobe! It's
just busy. I'm going to finish up all the
last minute details when I get home. I want
them to have a nice trip, first class!

"Hi, Sandy. I'm calling real quick before I go back on set. I hate that you can't fly out here with Sky and Zoey. Are you sure you can't?"

I wish I could, but I have to get this procedure done. I'm having a biopsy done because this cervical cancer thing is nothing to play with. You know I will be there with Mrs. Glover to see them off. I'm going to join you guys after I'm done. So we still will have a lot of fun."

"Yes, I know. I can't wait. Thank you again, Sandy, for being the best...the best friend anyone could ever dream of."

"Bitch, please. Don't go getting all mushy on me. Love you, Blu, like cooked food."

"Now why you had to go and compare me to food? With your greedy ass." We laughed off of that one.

Chapter Twenty-Two

The girls will be arriving at LAX at 1:55 pm, Los Angeles time. I'm standing here at gate forty-one. As a matter of fact, I'm so anxious and nervous I just couldn't sit at home. It's only 12:00 noon, but I know they in the air and I will be right here when that plane touch down. My new assistant, Paula, is a real sweetheart. My old assistant got a job working in New York City. I left Paula at the hotel to finish up everything I had put together for my girls. "Hey, Paula, how you coming along?"

"Hey. Everything is done, and I was on my way to wait with you."

"Okay, cool. See you when you get here. I'm at gate forty-one." I'm talking to Paula and I thought I heard my name on the P.A. system throughout the airport. Hold on a minute, because I thought I heard my name. Hold on Paula, my other line ringing, too. Hello?"

"Hi, Ms. Spencer. I am a representative on behalf of the airline, and we called your name on the P.A. in the airport. I wasn't sure if you're here, so that's why I'm calling."

"What's going on? Why would you be calling me?"

"Are you here at the airport, Ms. Spencer?"

"Yes! Yes, I'm at gate forty-one, waiting on my children."

"There is a TSA agent coming to meet you there now." The representative just hung up the phone so I clicked back and Paula was still there.

"Paula!"

"Yes, Blu. I'm here and I'm coming up the escalator now."

"Okay, but I have to go with security."

"Security! Why? I see you, Blu. Here I come." I saw a woman holding up a sign with my name on it. A man was standing next to her with an earpiece and holding a two-way radio.

Uneasily, I said, "I'm Ms. Spencer, and this is my assistant, Paula." They treated me with so much concern, but not telling me anything at the same time. It was now about 1:15 pm. We walked until we came to some elevators that were clearly not for the public to use. I was asked to wait in this private lounge. A handful of other people were sitting with concerned faces.

"Hello, Ms. Spencer. I'm Nancy McCall, but please call me Nancy. I'm the representative who spoke to you on the phone."

I asked in a very dull voice, "Nancy, where are my girls? Where is that airplane? Please don't give me no run around bullshit. I need to know! Where is that airplane?"

"Ms. Spencer, no one is able to explain what exactly happened at this point. Investigators will not make a final report until they've recovered the black boxes from the aircraft. Of the ninety-eight passengers and crew, there are believed to be no survivors. We don't know yet exactly where the plane disappeared. The plane's automatic communications system via satellite indicated the plane had experienced multiple technical failures during its last minutes in the air..." I stood there listening to this woman's voice sounding like it was echoing in my ears while she tells me in slow motion that my kids are dead. It was chaos in my head. What was I thinking...I made a huge error in judgment...all of the "would've, could've, should've" thoughts overwhelmed my mind. Nancy was still talking to me, but I could only hear the sound of my own heartbeat as if it were hooked to an ultrasound machine. I could hear Paula telling me to sit down. I closed my eyes, reminiscing on the day I gave birth to them. A chill runs through my body. My heart had a deep sharp pain that lasted until a numbness came over me. I sat in this lounge until the next day, waiting on that airplane to arrive. It had to be the afternoon when I saw my grandmother, my mom, and my two sisters and brother walk in the room. My other brother wasn't with them. I haven't talk to my siblings in a long time. I also see Thadius and his parents talking to Nancy. I can hear all sorts of representatives, officials, police, etc., all around me. All I can remember is my experience, giving birth to my babies. My mom is on one side of me and granma on the other. I feel something in my chest and my throat so if I speak I may just die. My kids are gone, vanished into thin air. No bodies, Nothing! Thadius and whoever interested can handle any and everything dealing with this nightmare. I don't care about the details or arrangements for Sky and Zoey. I'm not interested in a funeral of any kind with no evidence of my girls. They can do what they want to. My twins are dead. Do I even remember how to talk? I haven't said a word since I entered this lounge. I need to go home, but is that back to Georgia or my hotel here? I need to go wherever I can get a feeling and some kind of connection with my babies.

Chapter Twenty Three

I want to ask Paula how did I get in the bed? But I just laid in silence. "Blu, would you like to take a hot bath and get on some fresh pajamas?" I want to answer her but I can't. "Blu, can you hear me? Blu, please talk to me. I'm going to stay right here by your side."

"No! Go home, Paula, and turn that light off on your way out."

I woke up to a horrible migraine, also finding Paula still here laying on the sofa bed. "I'm sorry, Blu. I couldn't imagine leaving you."

In a soft, almost inaudible voice I said, "There must be a divine point to the tragedies in our lives...but then again, maybe the point is: there simply is no point."

I decided to get out of bed after seems like weeks. Mr.C is always having something delivered to brighten my day. He's even came out here a few times, if nothing else but be a shoulder to cry on. I'm back to business but I'm empty. My drive came from knowing I was making a better life for my girls and living out dreams of mine. Seventy-five percent of me wants to end it all but the other twenty-five says keep going.

Chapter Twenty Four

"**Ms. Spencer, it's** been almost two years.
Do you think you're ready to end our
sessions?"

"Well, shrink, what do you think?"

"I think by now you should be calling me
Angela."

"Okay, Angela."

"Thank you, Blu."

"Yeah, sure."

"Blu, you had a successful movie and success
beyond imagination. You will soon start
shooting your second movie. Your pictures
are in several magazines. Your career and
finances are in a good place right now, and
you and Cornelius have a beautiful home
right here in New York. However, your spirit
is down. Your joy and love for life is not

there. Don't get me wrong. I met you two weeks after the greatest tragedy a parent could experience. I expected far worse than what I saw in you. You have come a long way. You are no longer lifeless physically, but yet mentally you are carrying so much. Would you like to talk about any of that? I didn't really want to discuss what I'm feeling because I didn't know where to begin.

"Angela, I have a great support team. He's not just my husband, but Mr. C. is one of the greatest people I've ever met. Sandy is my very best friend in the whole world. Of course, there are others in my life who I love and respect as well. But those two are just as important as the air I breathe."

"That's great, Blu."

"Royce is a good friend of mine. He and his wife have a gorgeous son that's just like him. Most people know him as R.J. We all get together for special events and things like that."

"Okay, Blu. Let me be more specific. On any given day, do you normally feel sad, angry, hurt, or anything like that?

In a soft voice I said, "Yeah, every day. When I smile, it quickly turns into sadness because I feel that I shouldn't be smiling with all my loss. This emptiness consumes me. I haven't talked to Thadius, but then again, why would I? Our only connection was my girls, and they are gone. I do speak to Mrs. Glover periodically. However, doctor, on another note, I want to share with you today that I'm about six weeks pregnant. Nobody knows yet, not even Mr. C."

"Let me be the first to say congratulations."

"Thank you very much."

"My feelings are going crazy inside and I feel so empty."

"Okay, Blu, I would like to see you in one week. I want you to discontinue your antidepressants as of today. If you need me, please call and I will come to you, okay?"

"We've got to hurry, Blu. Everything is done. Now we need to get to the airport."

"Okay, I'm a little slow because I'm having some pains in my stomach along with fatigue. Relax, Paula, you been my assistant for a long time and I look at you like family now."

"Good, then I can comfortably say you need to tell your husband you are pregnant, number one. And number two, I don't think you should be going to L.A. right now discussing scripts for your new movie, having meetings and working as hard as you do. Oh, and did I mention, you don't feel well."

"Well, thank you, Paula, for the itinerary on what I should and shouldn't have. Now, let's go. I don't need to miss that plane."

Chapter Twenty Five

"**Paula, girl, it** sure feels good to have an apartment out here in sunny California. I'm here a lot, so hubby and I thought it made sense to get a spot. We spend so much money traveling until it's ridiculous but worth it. I'm back and forth between here and New York. Cornelius is between Atlanta, New York and LA. Anyway, Sandy should of got here yesterday. She is so particular about my wardrobe. I haven't heard from her, but she's not due here with me until first thing in the morning. Paula, order up some Chinese from my favorite place. You know what I like. I'm going to shower and relax, so bring it up when it gets here. "Okay and I'll bring up some tea with ginger as well, just the way you like it. Thanks Paula!

"Good morning, sleepyhead! You have a brunch meeting at ten thirty."

"Good morning, Paula. Blu, you were sleeping so peacefully last night so I didn't wake you to eat. After drinking my tea, it was over honey. Is Sandy here?"

"No, I called her last night to see when she would be here. It was no answer last night or this morning."

"What the hell? This is not like her at all. She emailed a few days ago and said she was leaving for Los Angeles and would see me soon. And now you can't get her on the phone at all, huh? Okay, well, leave her one more message and let's get me ready for this brunch meeting."

Chapter Twenty Six

"**Thank you for** calling Courtyard. May I help you?"

"I need to speak to Cornelius Hudson."

"Speaking. How may I help you?"

"Mr. C., this is Starr. Where is Blu?"

"She's in L.A. starting a new project. And to what do I owe the pleasure of this phone call?"

"Can you meet me for coffee?"

"Excuse me?"

Like I said, this is Starr and I need to talk to you, preferably in person. Now, again...

"Will you meet me for coffee?"

"No, but you can come to the hotel. What's going on, Starr, and why are you calling me?"

I will explain everything when I get there.

"I will be at your hotel in two hours."

Wow! What could Starr possibly want with me? Maybe I should call my wife and tell her about this shocking phone call. Let me see what's going on and I'll go from there.

"Hi, Starr, I see you're right on time. Now, what can I do for you?"

"Nothing, but Get Out Of My Way!" Two shots were fired. One in his chest, and then another in his head. This silencer on the gun really made a huge difference. I stood there for a second in disbelief, stunned at what I've just done, before running out the lobby doors, full speed! I threw my wig, clothes I was wearing, colored contacts, shoes and gun in different places on the way back to my condo.

I'm so nervous and feel sick to my stomach. I need to hurry and get out of this condo.

What is this man number? Oh, there it is.

"Hello. Yeah, I did it. It's done. By the way, I have her at one of the properties that just got put on the market. It's a new house with empty Lots around it that they have stopped building on so nobody is around. We have to take care of Sandy immediately."

You took the words right out of my mouth, Starr.

"So yes, take care of her then leave town. I will take it from here."

"R.J., I only got in on this with you because I know how you feel. I love Blu, too. I thought everybody was good with each other and have settled in their lives with the one they love. I see you have some unresolved issues that you never got over."

"I only made my move with someone else because Blu decided that her life would be better with the white dude."

"I feel you, R.J. That's why I want to get rid of Sandy. *I'm* her best friend, not this Sandy Bitch!"

"Starr, you are not her best friend. I know deep down you don't really care about Blu. I would consider you that silly ass word they call 'frienemy.' Look it up, and that's you. All right, go ahead and take care of that. When it's done, text me the number zero."

Chapter Twenty Seven

I don't know what the hell is going on. We've been in Los Angeles a whole week. Where the hell is Sandy? Mr. C. should be popping in any time now. When we've been apart, we love to give space so anticipation builds. I'm so in love with that man. He is heaven sent, and for all the right reasons.

I feel so weak. I was spotting yesterday, and the doctor told me over the phone to get in a couple of days bed rest, then come see him. I'm waiting for my hubby so he can get the news that he's going to be a daddy while we on the way to see the doctor. I decided not to wait until we got back to New York. My feet are up, so I probably should go over some scripts. I just can't concentrate though.

"Paula, did you order food? I need to slow my greedy ass down."

"No, I didn't think you wanted anything to eat yet. Relax, I'll get the door."

"Good afternoon. We're looking for Mrs. Blu Spencer-Hudson." Just a minute, leaving the gentlemen at the door, I turned to get Blu, but she was already standing there. "We are homicide detectives from Atlanta, Georgia."

Blu said, "Step in and let's have a seat in the front room."

"Yes, ma'am. We regret to inform you that your husband..." I heard nothing after husband. Any sound of a voice fell on deaf ears at that point. I instantly felt like I was standing in that airport two years ago when my babies just vanished into thin air. "Ma'am, can you hear me?"

In a sad voice, I said, "Yes, I can hear you."

"You will need to come back to Atlanta to take care of the technicalities. Here is my card. Call us once you get to town. Sorry for your loss."

When I looked up about two seconds later, Paula had tears in her eyes. In disgust I said, "I'm taking my hubby back to New York and bury him. The South is not it for me. I'm going to sell all ten hotels and all his other endeavors down there. It's all estimated to be millions. I'm going to sell our house in New York. I'm thinking of going out of the country for a while. I will keep this apartment but everything else goes. He never got the chance to know he was going to be a father. In my head I just keep repeating, *where is Sandy? I need you, girl.*

Where are you? Each day is definitely presenting its own struggle. The caller I.D. is showing Starr's number.

"Hello."

"Hey, Blu. I just got word about what happen. Do they know any details on what happen?"

"No. Just a woman shot him and left the hotel."

"Do you think he might've been sleeping around? Having an affair or something?" I just hung up on that stupid bitch.

My accountants, everybody, my whole team took care of and is still taking care of all my business. "Paula, thank god everything is wrapping up so quickly. My goodness, I'm so tired and feeling fatigued."

"Well, you are pregnant, Blu, and you just lost your husband."

"Cornelius had very specific instructions on what to do when he passed on. I hate it, but he was cremated just as he requested. I'm holding on to my baby for dear life. I'm trying to stay calm as I can. Speaking of the baby, Paula, I thank you for getting with my doctor and finding me the perfect doctor in Italy. Although I'm not from there, my roots are there. My grandmother was born there, and so was my mom, but they moved here when Cora was a toddler. Excuse me, for just a minute, Paula. R.J.'s wife is calling me on my cell phone. Hi, Beverly."

"Hey angel face."

"Oh, R.J., I thought you were wifey."

"I'm calling for her. She wants to meet with you at your favorite spa tomorrow. It's all on me. Anything you girls want, the sky is the limit." R.J. didn't say anything about Mr. C., and neither did I because I don't want to talk about "ANYTHING" concerning my husband. "It's too much!" Let Beverly know I will meet her at the spa.

What the hell is R.J. doing here? Of course, I'm looking for Beverly to be here at the spa. I thought he and I had gotten past all that was between us. I thought we settled everything and was in a good, respectful place with one another.

"Okay, so where is Beverly?"

"All bullshit aside, I needed to see you."

"And why?"

"Because I needed to see."

I had no reason not to trust him, so when he extended his hand, I grabbed it and let him lead me all the way back out of the spa to the car. I didn't open my mouth while he led me... until we were in a hotel room. He whispered in my ear, "Let neither one of us say a word." I continued to stay silent as he hugged and caressed me the way I remember. R.J. hasn't changed a bit. He smells so good. I feel the tension leaving my body as he gently squeezed my shoulders while kissing my neck.

"Stop! Please, Just Stop! I'm grieving and pregnant with my husband's baby."

"Pregnant? Are you serious?"

"Yes, very serious, and very pregnant."

"Sit down, Blu." I sat and watched him while he messed around with his laptop. Before I knew it, he was on Skype, and Starr was on his screen talking to him. The only thing that came to mind was, *what the fuck is going on?*

"Starr, move to the side so Blu can see her folks."

"Oh my god, that's Sandy."

"Sit down and be quiet like I asked you to do the first time, Blu. All right, Starr, one to the chest and then one to the head. Do it the same as before."

"You had Starr kill my husband, R.J.?

And now my friend?"

I heard a gunshot but didn't look at the screen. I tried to run out the door but he caught the bottom of my shirt and snatched me backwards. The room was silent outside of us scuffling. I looked at the computer. It was fuzzy with no picture. I was on my stomach on the bed, exhausted and breathing hard. My body was still. This is not the R.J. I met and thought I knew.

As he stroked my hair, in a calm, creepy voice, he said, "I love you, and I don't want to hurt you. Please believe me, baby. I'm sorry for even manhandling you that way, but you have to understand that what you found out here today must stay with you. Meaning, your granma means the world to you. Am I correct?" I took a deep breath, knowing exactly where he was coming from.

"What's the reason for all this? What was the point in killing my husband and my best friend? They were everything to me."

"You just answered your own questions in a nut shell. You are one of the most beautiful, naturally talented women in the world. But you chose someone else, after it was all said and done. So they had to go. Point blank. Period."

"I asked you long ago, R.J., before all the money and fame, why were you doing all of this for me and at what cost. You said you had all you needed and you just knew a good talent and wanted to help me out because I could never get connected with the right people on my own. No strings attached! Those were your words, R.J. The life of the people I love is the price for you helping me? Like I always said, nothing is free, and that's very clear to me now." I'm laying here with this fool snuggled up behind me as if everything is all right. I'm trying to hold my emotions and tongue in check until I can figure out how I'm getting out of here. R.J. assured me that when I leave don't forget that I know nothing about he and Starr killing Mr. C. or the consequences would be great, starting with my granma.

"So, when is this supposed to happen?" he asked, pointing at my stomach.

"I'm only a couple of months or so. Is Sandy dead?"

"The bitch better be, or Starr is going to have a problem."

Again, holding my emotions and tongue, I said, "Will you please let me go?"

"Sure, and I will be over to your place when I tie up all my loose ends with all this bullshit." As I was leaving the hotel, R.J. said, "Sorry for your loss."

I stood silent for a minute, and then repeated, "Will you let me go?"

He said, "Bye," in a dismissing tone.

Chapter Twenty Eight

Paula must be out on some errands. I
want so bad to conquer this breakdown that I
feel slowly moving in on me. Pregnant and
all, I still had to self-medicate so I could
go to sleep. It's close to 1 am, and the
T.V. is unusually loud with the newscaster
saying, "Breaking news! Woman shot twice—
once in the chest and once in the head. An
unidentified woman was left for dead in a
newly built upscale subdivision. Report says
she is in critical condition. Stay tuned for
further updates on this breaking story. I
threw my hands up in a gesture of surrender
to the most high. Father, save my friend. I
plead to you, God, to not only save her, but
also restore her head and body back to being
able to function on their own. Oh my God,

give me strength to go to her, in spite of my own unwelcome life challenges.

I caught the next flight out. My face etched with concern, I walked toward Sandy's bed. She was wrapped like a mummy and had tubes coming from everywhere. In the days and weeks that followed, Sandy surprisingly was improving. Detectives, both undercover and uniformed, were hanging around. Two officers were interviewing or should I say interrogating anybody who came to visit her. Once I told them who I was, they began to share with me that it's a possible connection between my husband and Sandy's shooting. They told me they had some leads but nothing concrete that they could share.

I want to tell them, Yes, I know who did this awful thing, and Yes, I can take you straight to them. Why can't I just tell them and let them protect my granma. I want to, I need to, I just can't. Today would be my last day here. I whispered in Sandy's ear and squeezed her hand. I turned toward the door and headed straight to the airport. I can't come back here to Atlanta. I'm not ready.

"Good afternoon, Ms. Spencer. How are you and baby feeling today? I'm so sorry for your loss. My condolences to you and your family. A lot has happened in such a short amount of time." The doctor held my hand and said again, "I'm so sorry, and my heart goes out to you. We need to get you set up for an ultrasound."

After telling my doctor about these cramping episodes, nausea, and the spotting of blood, he wanted to do everything an entire exam entailed right away. I told him, "Let's take care of everything first thing in the morning. One more day won't make a difference, will it doctor?"

"I suppose not, Ms. Spencer, however, I'm concerned about your symptoms and we need to know what's going on so we can treat you accordingly."

"Okay, okay. I hear you, and I will see you first thing in the morning."

He said with a smirk, but I-mean-business face, "Go get off your feet. Doctor's orders, young lady."

How was your doctor's appointment, Blu?

"You don't look like yourself at all."

"Well, it's me. What do I look like?"

"More like a knock-off, rather than the real thing." Was this Paula's way of breaking the ice in this cold, bleak apartment?

"Just kidding, It's just you are so beautiful and ..."

"Yeah, well...considering...I hope to pull it all back together. Hopefully!"

"Hello?"

"What's up, angel face? What are you doing? Are you home?" I only had dead silence to offer this man. "How about opening the door?"

"Since you knew I was home, why ask?"

"I have to go out of town, so pack a bag. You going with me."

"I consider myself already out of town because I live in New York."

"You have an apartment here in L.A., so this home, too. Now, pack a bag, or it can be like old times, if you want, I can buy what you need once we get there." This man had Starr of all people murder my husband and attempt to murder my best friend, who is fighting for her life. R.J. is acting like it's all non-existent to say the least. Numbness is an understatement. I don't feel anything, not even fear. Part of me, or maybe even all of me, wants to lie down and go to sleep never to wake.

"Take this pill, Blu."

"No, I can't. I'm pregnant."

What kind of pill is this? Angel face, it won't put you to sleep, completely and it won't hurt you or your baby so don't worry about what kind it is. I'm not taking something and don't know what it is R.J ok. Is that right? He pushed three pills down my throat making me gag. If you throw-up I'ma make you take them again and you're not going to know what they are so let it go.

" See, baby, I don't mean to scream at you or get hostile. Just do as I say and everything will go smoothly."

I'm so tired and very weak. I've been spotting. We have been traveling from car to plane, now in another car. I'm extremely weak. I see and hear R.J. explaining to people that I'm ill, but I can't speak or anything. I have a pad on and it's soaked with blood. I see a sign that says,

"Welcome to Edinburgh in Paris, London."

The cab we riding in, pulls around back of a building that looks like a small abandoned castle. A woman comes to the car, helps R.J. take me inside. R.J. undresses me with the help of the lady with white hair.

"Damn, Blu. Your clothes are covered in blood." I'm so weak, I can hardly move.

The lady says, "Turn her over. Pull her up in the bed. She's shaking, put another blanket on her."

Hello, You are very weak. I will be assisting R.J in caring for you. I'm known as Ma'am, that's what you can call me. This is my home and no need to be afraid, you are safe here. Get some rest and I will check on you later.

"Wake up, Blu. You need to eat. You've been in and out of sleep for days." R.J. is treating me with care and concern in a bizarre, weird way. He did a little chuckle laugh and said, "We belong together". I had to remove anybody that would stop that. I hope you understand. Let me sit you out on the veranda so you can get some air. No words, I sat in silence. I have some things to do so Ma'am will check on you later. Two ladies, four children and a baby are on the other side of this brown wood fence. I don't know where the lady with the white hair is and R.J. left. I walked as fast as I could over to the fence.

"Hi. Can I talk to you?"

In a strong English accent, the woman said, "Walk to the end of the fence and through the gate."

"I need help. I was brought here from the States unknowingly and unwillingly. Can I come in your house, please? Maybe you can help me. I have money."

"Madam, what is your name?"

"Blu. Blu Spencer. I'm pregnant and I'm sick. I want to go home and I can't go back to the house next door. I need to call my assistant back in the states. She will send for me and any money you need."

The lady took me in and after dark we went to the airport. She told me, God Be With You, Child, and left.

After telling Paula everything that I could possibly remember, I told her we're probably going to have to leave L.A. sooner than later.

"I didn't report anything because you left with R.J. I thought you were fine. Now that you have told me everything, Blu, we have to leave here immediately. Did he say anything about Starr's whereabouts?"

"No."

"I'm sorry to tell you this, but Sandy died last week." Tears filled my eyes. Chest pains came out of nowhere. I sat at the table and thought about me and Sandy's whole relationship from the first day I met her, my water breaking and knocking on her door for help. I can't speak out loud about her death. My mind is overflowing with thoughts of her. "Blu..."

"What is it, Paula?"

"Are you going to the police about Starr and R.J. and tell them everything that has gone on?"

"Did you get my granma straight?"

"Yes, I did."

"Paula, I pray they both rot in hell, but I have to leave and don't know when I'll return."

"I've never been to Italy."

"Neither have I, but it's a fresh start for me and my baby. I'll see that doctor as soon as we get there."

Chapter Twenty Nine

"**Where are we** going? I have a plane to catch!"

"You fainted, ma'am, and we're taking you to the nearest hospital. Are you her family?"

"Yes, I am. My name is Paula."

"I'm Dr. Tally. Ms. Spencer's obstetrician was contacted and he will be here as soon as he can. The information you gave us was very helpful."

"Is she okay, doctor?"

"We discovered that she had an ectopic pregnancy, meaning that the baby was developing in her fallopian tube."

"What do you mean, *had*?"

"Ms. Spencer had to undergo emergency surgery. She had a lot of damage, so we had to perform a hysterectomy. Unfortunately, her bowel was perforated during the surgery, and we had to insert an N.G. tube into her stomach. Because of the nick to her small intestine, she may require an ileostomy bag, but for now we are monitoring her closely and doing everything that can be done."

"How in the hell did you cut her damn intestines open?"

"Because of all the scarring and damage, her bowel was nicked." He just kept repeating the same thing, never really saying anything. This doctor is talking like the cut in her bowel just appeared during surgery. Yes, she had issues with scarring, damage and all that other shit! Undoubtedly the scar tissue came from previous pregnancies. However, a slip of the hand, and somebody cut her up on the inside.

"When can I see her?"

"She's in recovery and will be moved to the surgical floor once she wakes up. I will talk more with you in a few days, but if you have any questions, the nurse will contact me for you. Good day."

As her assistant, I guess I should contact Ms. Lena because I don't know which way this is going to turn. We not at the house in New York or the apartment here, so we safe and won't be found. What am I saying? That house is sold in New York. I'm going to get a hotel room by the hospital and go back and forth for now.

The first month went by, the second, and then the third. The nurses were phenomenal. Most of them had seen me on T.V. or in a magazine. I forgot through everything who I was.

"Debbie, you are my favorite nurse."

"And you are my favorite patient. Mainly because you have such a positive attitude and always trying hard as you can to get better."

"I'm sorry, Ms. Spencer. You have to be prepped for surgery right now."

"AGAIN!"

"It's okay," Blu, I'm your nurse and will be right here with you.

"Your bowel is obstructed, meaning that the contents of the intestine can't pass through." The surgeon continued, "We're going to fit you with an ileostomy bag. This will allow waste to come out through a surgical cut in your stomach."

"Count backwards from ten, Blu."

My eyes popped open like they were on a timer. I felt the presence of someone standing on the left side of my bed so I turned my head just a little to see who it was. R.J stood there with a smirk on his face looking like he was waiting on me to wake all the way up. Even though I was on a ventilator, my mind was telling me I was suffocating. I felt a cold chill go down my neck and back. My eyes started watering. I'm not sure if I'm scared or angry. I laid in disbelief , thinking how in the hell does he know where I am? He has taken everything so what does he want? I don't think he was trying to kill me in London, at least not yet! Oh God! Did he come to do it now? I looked him in his eyes until he started to talk and I immediately close them.

"Good morning, angel face. Did you think I wouldn't be able to find you? I explained to Paula what's what, so she is on board, not that she has a choice. I told her she's welcome to continue coming to visit you. I think she understands everything. If you need to say something, just write on the notepad. I know that has to be terrible being on a ventilator. The doctor said after surgery you still had trouble breathing on your own. Damn, girl! You're wearing a bag and you on a respirator. Because you in critical condition, I'm letting it slide how you slipped away from me in London." I'll let you rest. I'm gone, for now. I opened my eyes now that he's gone and called for the nurse. She gave me some meds because I was in distress.

I'm so happy to be out of that hospital. The fresh air smells so good. The sun shining, birds singing and people out and about everywhere.

Although I'm weak and wearing this bag, I have a I.V in my arm because I have to administer fluids to myself and take medications many times a day but I am here! The good Lord is keeping me here for something. At the end of this seemingly never-ending nightmare, I have to stay strong. "Paula, you have really stuck by me, girl.

"I'm not going anywhere, Blu. I'm glad you home. We're going to get through this, too. When you were in the hospital, I know what R.J. told me, but I'm not even worried about him."

"He is a devil in disguise. When I was in the hospital God came and sat with me. He never left me and he told me to let him deal with Starr and R.J. He said give him all of my loss, shame and guilt because it's too big for me. So, one day I gave it all to him. I haven't seen R.J. for a while, and with me getting ready to go live in Italy, I feel like I can take my first deep breath."

"Blu, how does it feel to know they're making a movie about your life?"

"I have only two words to answer that: It's unbelievable. With me not being able to work again, is real hurtful. Just the activity of daily living on my own terms is a wrap. I'm extremely weak because my body won't retain fluids. I have to empty this ileostomy bag every forty-five minutes to an hour. The output is horrendous, and when it puts out too much and my body gets depleted of fluids, I faint. My body locks up and shuts down until I can get a good amount of fluids restored back in my body. The list goes on. I've been changed forever."

"The two live-in nurses you hired will help ease the pain of it all."

"It is so beautiful in Italy."

"Yes it is, Blu, and this house is like a picture book. You have two nurses, a chef, housekeepers, grounds men and security like I've never seen before."

"I wish I had someone to stand in my place with this body. No amount of money can change this. My stomach is wide open, healing from the inside out. I have a bag on the side that has to be emptied every hour. The nurse has to pack my open wound with special gauze twice a day until it heals. I try to verbally express how I feel, but there really are no words."

"Why is his name Gomez, and he is black?" Me and Paula laugh while we sat at the table and ate. "He is a great chef, no matter what his name is, Paula. Too bad I eat like a bird now. This bag still gives me fits. Sadie, thank you for finding little ways to keep this bag from leaking, it's hell."

"Ms. Blu, we're your nurses, and it's our job to do what we're doing."

Well, I love my entire staff.

"I'm saying thank you because you need to know how you have changed our lives. We are all here for you, and yet you have afforded us lifestyles we could only imagine."

"You're welcome!" With a smile on my face, I softly said, "Now, go find yourself something to do, Sadie. Coming in here with all that sentimental junk."

I have hibernated long enough. I haven't had to go back in the hospital and I've put on a few pounds. "You've come a long way, Ms. Blu, but you still have just as far, if not further to go."

"Why can't you be a quiet nurse like Ms. Marsha? Seriously, Sadie, I'm going to open a club here. Build it from the ground. Paula has already gotten with the right people so we can make this happen."

"What kind of club are you opening?"

"The type of club I could always see myself in years ago. The type of club I used to fantasize about. Something that was once a dream, meaning *me* being the H.B.I.C.!" We laughed hard on that. "Now I can make my dream a reality. This is going to be my pastime, especially with me being in my predicament. I'm starting with one club here in Italy and one in Philadelphia."

"Why Philly?"

"Paula is from there, among other reasons. When you go downstairs, tell Paula I need to see her.

 Seems like everything coming along with the clubs."

"Yes, they are absolutely beautiful. Although in construction, I see what they going to look like from the floor plans." So, Blu, I'm puzzled by the name.

"The Entertaining May Spot, coming soon!"

"Why are you calling it that?"

"And what's wrong with that?"

"Oh, nothing at all. It's odd, and I don't know what it means."

"It comes from the word Maypole. That's a long pole with ribbons at the top but cancel the ribbons honey, we not doing that."

"The women who work there will be my protégées. It's going to be more than a club. Outside of being one of the most prestigious clubs you can work at, there will be benefits for you and your children. If you got the look, body and personality, you can and will go straight to the top."

"Oh my God, Blu. I see that everything is handcrafted. You had the furniture made just for each club and you very particular about the food."

"I know. I'm really excited about it. I have more money than I could ever spend. Between me and my husband, money is not at all a factor. True, it's going to make money, but I'm doing it for the enjoyment."

"Blu, if I ask you something, you promise you won't be mad?"

"What?"

"You don't ever speak about Sky and Zoey. Do you go through something when you think about them?"

"When I look back over my life, what I feel is overwhelming. I've learned not to try to understand everything. Some things probably will never make sense. To answer your question, I used to go through something. I had my own private goodbye in my heart for them. I found this poem written by Marin McKay and for some unexplainable reason, it helps me feel connected to them. Every day, since we've been living here, I recite this poem to them in my mind."

"Can I hear it?"

"Ummm, okay.

I think of you girls every day. You probably don't realize how important you were to me. There are times when the one thing that helps me get through the day...is thinking of you. Thoughts of you bring me happiness when my world seems to be wearing a frown. When things don't quite go as planned and my world is upside down, thoughts of you help to set things right again. You were so important to me. You made me think, you made me laugh, you made me feel alive and you are where I drew my purpose from. You provided automatic support and encouragement. You lessen my worries and increase my joy for life. If my life were a puzzle, you would be the two pieces that make a perfect fit. Every day I think of you both. I got a heart full of love and a mind full of memories to prove it."

"Blu, you are the strongest person I have ever met."

"You always say that, Paula! Okay, let's eat. What do you have a taste for?"

"Nothing with pasta in it, please!"

"Let's be clear. There's a difference between pasta and Cup--noodles. Paula, you eat noodles like it's a medication you have to take everyday." I laughed while holding my stomach. Paula wasn't amused.

Let's go see the club. It's Up so now it's time to get it running!

"This is beautiful. I don't even want to use the term 'strip club' in the same sentence with "The Entertaining May Spot!" Wow. It's amazing in here. They have done a remarkable job. It's everything I dreamed and then some. Certain areas of the club have mirrors that are images of a woman. This place has four fantasy rooms. Two rooms are Pandora's boxes, and the other two are exclusive V.I.P. There's an area for general V.I.P. and, of course, lavish sofas for conversation, beautiful mahogany tables with high-backed chairs and tall stools with legs carved in feminine form. So many other amenities that would take forever to name. No pool tables or games of any kind. It's strictly about the ladies in here. I am pleased. I want to thank everybody for your hard work in making this dream of a club into a reality." Especially you, Paula. You have been my right hand. Thank you, so very much!

Chapter Thirty

"**Dr. Tally, I** am nervous about this ileostomy reversal."

"Your bowel had to rest and you get stronger. I think you're as ready as you're ever going to be. We're basically putting your bowel back together. You will no longer have the bag. If it's successful, your bowel should function in the regular way. You'll have a period of adjustment, but you can do it." We are going to take good care of you.

"Ms. Spencer, the reversal was a success, however you have to have the N.G. tube again, and you must be on this ventilator until you are stronger. Your heart rate is slow and your blood pressure is high. You have an infection in your lower abdomen. We have inserted a drain in your stomach and one in your lower pelvic area to drain an abscess." Every day is a challenge in here but I'm so happy the doctor said I can go home in a few days. For the last couple of days I'm under observation before being discharged.

Paula, I know I'm starting to sound like a broken record, when I say I'm glad to be home.

"I'm really happy to be home. Those forty-five days in the hospital seemed like forty-five years. All the dancers, employees and people who wished me well were so supportive. Soon as I feel up to it, I'm going to open a club in a couple of other cities, just not sure where yet. So many entrepreneurs are trying to meet with me. People admire my establishments. Paula, you have made me your whole life. Don't you think about dating, sex and so on?"

"Do you?"

"No, not really. With all my tragedies and illnesses, I don't think about it at all. What I do think about is all the money I been paying this man to find Starr."

"So, what are you saying, Blu? Has he found her?"

"Yes, he has and he is right on point with wheeling her right on in. I've been working on this little project for a while." Guy went to Atlanta, started dating Starr and they have been an item for a while. He easily persuaded her to come to Philly. When the market crash with real estate her funds took a turn for the worst. Starr went back to her roots of dancing so that made my plans for her fit like a hand in a glove.

She was already on a downward spiral being back on the dust and drinking heavily.

"Does she still have dealings with Thadius?"

"Don't know. I have no ties with anyone from my past. It doesn't matter either way because my guy is a genius at what he does. She is already coming to Philly on a regular basis with him. Everything is on time, as planned. You answered my question with a question. Paula, do you think about a man? Sex and so on?"

"Yes, I've seen someone that I looked twice at. I actually think about Lennox."

"Who the hell is that?"

"He is your chief of security."

"Oh Damn! Sure is. We run a tight ship and you know better than anyone that there is no fraternizing on the job. You have to venture out, honey. Paula, you are a cute, dainty something."

"Well, thank you, I think."

"I miss Ms. Marsha because she was a very attentive, caring nurse, however I don't miss why she was here in the first place. My stomach is still so very sore, and where that bag was, it hasn't closed yet. Sadie takes good care of me. When it comes to all this G.I. stuff, she knows her business. Did you send Ms. Marsha and her family the gifts I picked out for them?"

"Yes."

"Did you make sure they got them?"

"Yes."

"Were they pleased? I really appreciated her"

"Yes, yes, and yes."

"Hand me the phone, Paula."

"Hello?"

"Hi, Guy."

"Just a little update for you."

"I'm listening."

"She is to the point where she wants some blow every day. Starr works at your club and I got her some private appointments every night."

"Good! Keep her on dayshift so she won't miss the setups at night." Guy is so serious about his job in the disposal business.

He said, "I'll be in touch," and hung up. I laid down for a while, and when I woke up it was the next day. I went to the club as usual. I stayed until I was content with knowing what's going on with everything. I have a staff that couldn't get any better. They were all carefully screened and selected. My club in Philly is run the same way. I just had to sit back in my chair and take a deep breath. My mind is overflowing with the details of another club I'm opening. Lennox, My head security guy is walking around here looking intimidating as usual. He won't look me in my eyes because he's not sure what I know about him and Paula. As I sit in my office, I can't help but wonder how long they been messing around. I haven't seen anything but my gut feeling is telling me something is between those two. I will deal with that later.

I have an appointment at four o'clock. Its four fifteen, so where is this woman. I'm interviewing for an attendant to do just what the name says—attend to the dancers making sure they have everything they need. She will have her own office that sits off from the dressing rooms.

"Nice to meet you. My name is Seven. I'm Blu, and it's nice to meet you, but you're late. After I told her how serious punctuality is. I, rather we, do take it seriously. I start talking about the job. You will have a base salary, however the ladies can—and more than likely will—tip you if they want to. As I continued explaining the job description I sipped on hot tea with ginger and shuffled through the mail that the housekeeper gave me on my way here this morning. Seven shared some of her ideas, and a few of them were quite impressive. Who could this letter be from with no return address and written by hand? We wrapped up the meeting and, compared with the other prospects, Seven seemed like she just might be the one. I can't wait for Lennox to come see her out so I can open this envelope. Seven and I shook hands and she left.

Greetings,

I was one of the attending physicians who flew to Italy during your ileostomy reversal. I am chief of radiology. I asked a superior medical colleague what he thought about me contacting you, and he saw no harm in it. I insert drains pertaining to abscesses, infections in the abdomen, etc. I hope you are well and thriving back to your activity of daily living. I will be out there in a couple of weeks. If this letter found you then please contact me. My information is at the bottom of the page. It would be an honor to see you again.

Be well,

Dr. Moore

I folded the letter put it in my purse, leaned back in my chair and said to myself, Hhmmmmm, I haven't had a man show kindness and genuine interest in a long time. Scary but nice. I left the club with a smile, telling myself, I may just contact him.

 I haven't eaten all day other than drank that tea. "Gomez, do you mind making me a salad? Add spinach and chicken, please."

"Absolutely, coming right up!"

"If anyone needs me, I'll be in the theater." I got my salad and lemonade, watched a movie and went to bed later that night.

"Blu, it's been over a week and you just been up here in this room. Are you feeling all right?"

"Don't start worrying, Paula. I'm sure it's more mental than physical. I have a great team, so my world is safely ran smoothly. Right?"

"Right!"

"I have to fly to Philadelphia tomorrow and I need you to get my things together. I will only be gone a few days. You stay and mind things around here. You have Coppia here, and you know I recently added to her duties. She is not just the housekeeper. She's a very smart woman. I was surprised at a lot of things once I got to know her. Coppia is very business savvy."

"How was your flight, Ms. Spencer?"

"Long! Will you have some hot tea with ginger brought to my room please?"

"Anything else?"

"No, not right now."

"The bell hop will be along with your luggage shortly. Enjoy your stay, Ms. Spencer."

First order of business is to go to the club. I arrange for Sadie to have her own room. I'm not entirely well, so it's important that my nurse be with me. She stays on schedule with her nurse duties. From checking my blood pressure to giving my meds and keeping a close eye on me so I don't overdo it. She's good!

After my staff meeting at the club, I went on a retreat at one of the most upscale spas in Philly. While relaxing I was interrupted by my never stop-ringing phone. "This is Blu."

"Yeah, like I told you the other day, Starr overdosed and is in some county hospital."

"Hello to you, too."

"This is business. I don't deal in charismatic behavior. Period. I will be picking her up tomorrow. I'm ready to close what's left of my deal with you."

"Okay, you will get the last part of your money when it's done."

"Ms. Spencer, would you like me to relight the candles?"

"No! They were giving me a headache. That's why I blew them out."

"That particular aroma may be too strong for you."

"Charge it to my account, I need a longer foot rub."

I feel like I've slept a long time, this woman was still rubbing my feet. She said it's called a foot reflexology massage. I'm going back to the club to wrap things up, and then back to Italy.

No sooner than I can get settled in at home, I got a call from Guy saying when he picked Starr up and took her home, she and another dancer was getting high. The dancer left, but Starr shot herself a lethal dose of heroin. She was dead on the kitchen floor when he walked in. "Yeah so, since I didn't have to make that final move on her, the funds change."

"Meaning what, Guy?"

"You owe less."

"Well, I want to pay what I promised, because I need you to look a little harder into finding R.J. I know you did this for me before, but it's just strange how he fell off the earth. He was this big time producer. He got me started in this business, where could he be? Someone will put your money in the safe deposit box in the same place. Contact me if you find anything out on R.J."

"Will do." And we both hung up.

I want to hate Starr so bad right now. I'm not going to go into some shell having deep thoughts about the woman who killed my husband and best friend in cold blood. That bitch deserved to die a slow death.

The Entertaining May Spot will be opening in two more cities real soon. Directors in Hollywood want me to come back to work. The magazines want me to do a spread on "Life after Loss, Depression and Illness." People want to hear my story. It just goes to show: through it all, "the darkness and the pain, the storms and the rain," when the sun comes out, I can see "Blu is in the Rainbow, Too!"

Blu is in the Rainbow, Too!

Kimberly Bell

Acknowledgements

To the Most High: Thank You for my Life. To my Children: Devin, Darien & DeAndre I love you with all my heart. To my Mom: Thank you P.T. for being there through it all,

your only child loves you. To * Renae Baldwin *Penny Turner *Shawnda minor *Gayla Woodson *Sada Woodson *Carla Wright *Ayuna Terrell *Dephanie North *Tonya Tabious *Danita Franklin *Taurus Woodley *Nekatana Gilliam *Anjenette Gilliam *Erika Smith *Jasmine Haley *Tyesha Weaver *Briana Bolt *Deyana Clay and *Benita Minor, you were the first to read my manuscript. You gave constructive criticism and a lot of support. I thank each and every one of you for caring about me.

To my readers/fans: Thank you so much for ALL of your support.

Author's Notes

This book is a work of fiction. Names, characters, places and events are solely the product of the author's imagination. Any similarities to any individuals living or dead, is entirely coincidental.

ISBN-13: 978-0-615-96341-9

Copyright © Kimberly Bell, 2013

Editor: Alycia Metz

Graphic Designer: Jacob Mason